THUNDER TO THE WEST

There had been no trouble until Curt O'Dion came along. Claiming to be the new owner of Quirt and Slash Y, the big outfits in the valley of the Bitter Sage, he never explained what had happened to the former owner. He didn't feel he had to explain his plans to take over the whole region either. But Brick Gordon, a Quirt rider, was not bothered about obligations; open warfare, in the form of a hail of bullets soon persuaded him to mosey over the Slash with his services. O'Dion thought he was safe: Gordon must be a dead man, but he had to think again when he saw the enemies' new ramrod, intent on revenge . . .

THUNDER TO
THE WEST

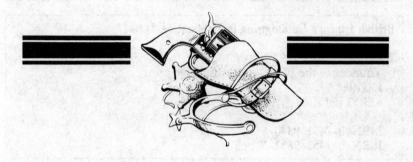

Lynn Westland

ATLANTIC LARGE PRINT
Chivers Press, Bath, England.
Curley Publishing, Inc.,
South Yarmouth, Mass., USA.

Library of Congress Cataloging-in-Publication Data

Westland, Lynn, 1899–
   Thunder to the west / Lynn Westland.
     p. cm.—(Atlantic large print)
   Previously published under the pseudonym Al Cody.
   ISBN 0–7927–0300–6 (soft: lg. print)
   1. Large type books. I. Title.
   [PS3519.O712T5 1990]
   813′.52—dc20   90–32695
                                                CIP

British Library Cataloguing in Publication Data

Westland, Lynn, *1899–*
   Thunder to the West.—(Atlantic large print).
   I. Title
   813.52 [F]

   ISBN 0–7451–9840–6
   ISBN 0–7451–9852–X pbk

This Large Print edition is published by Chivers Press, England, and Curley Publishing, Inc, U.S.A. 1990

Published by arrangement with Donald MacCampbell, Inc.

U.K. Hardback ISBN 0 7451 9840 6
U.K. Softback ISBN 0 7451 9852 X
U.S.A. Softback ISBN 0 7927 0300 6

© Copyright 1964, by Arcadia House

Photoset, printed and bound in Great Britain by
REDWOOD PRESS LIMITED, Melksham, Wiltshire

CHAPTER ONE

Brick Gordon's mood was evil, his temper short, and he was well aware of it. He glanced toward O'Rourke's Saloon, seeing it as a symbol of the change which was sweeping the country, finding in it an added cause for irritation. It was about time for a man like himself to be moving on to a new range.

The transformation of O'Rourke's Saloon was just about complete. Inside, carpenters were still sawing and hammering, but on the outside it was newly painted, the color a garish pink which was an affront to the eyes as well as to the sensibilities. A sign, bearing the name 'Grand Theatre,' had just been erected, replacing the name of O'Rourke. Culture was coming to Long Rain, bestowed upon it by the largesse of Curt O'Dion; a sort of forced feeding, as was true of everthing done by the boss of Quirt.

Gordon shrugged, wavering between amusement and disgust. He'd been with O'Dion a couple of months before, riding into town along with Felix Yankus and Monte Yuma. It was not by chance, as they and everyone recognized, that O'Dion chose the three best gunslingers when he took his rides. It had been that day, he guessed, that the idea for the theatre had come to O'Dion.

1

At the time, there had been two saloons in town: The Silver Dollar, patronized by Quirt, and O'Rourke's, favored by the riders from Slash Y. Only the week before, by some deal undisclosed to the general public, O'Dion had acquired control of The Silver Dollar.

Then, instead of entering his own saloon, he'd headed for the rival establishment, with the trio at his heels, startling O'Rourke by their appearance. That had been nothing compared to what followed. O'Dion had ordered a drink and downed it; then he'd coolly informed O'Rourke that he was buying him out.

The declaration had been as much of a surprise to Gordon as to O'Rourke; it still left a bad taste in his mouth, as he thought back and remembered the dismayed helplessness of the paunchy big man, forced to sell at a ruinous price. There had been no overt show of force; the guns of Quirt were persuasion enough, even when they remained holstered. O'Rourke had indulged in one bleat of complaint.

'But what do you want with another saloon, O'Dion?' What about the place you already have? And where will Slash Y go for its drinks?'

'Now that is a good question.' Curt Dion had stroked his silky mustache and smiled. 'As to what I want with it—' He'd made up a high-sounding answer on the spur of the moment, since his pride would not admit to the bald truth: that he wanted to force all competition out of business.

'It's not as a liquor dispensary that I'm interested in the building, O'Rourke. Not that at all. What runs in my mind is that Long Rain should have an opera house of its own, a classy place for entertainment.' Liking the notion, he had pursued it enthusiastically.

'Why should we, here at the county seat, take a back seat to such an upstart town as New Cheyenne, which boasts such entertainment and makes slighting remarks about us? You, my friend, will be hailed as a public-spirited benefactor for having donated this building for such a purpose!'

Bitter but helpless, O'Rourke had not remained to watch the transformation of the saloon into a theatre. He was gone, like the many others who had crossed O'Dion's path or simply happened to be in his way.

A large hand-bill, printed on pink paper, had been tacked to the board fence adjacent to the former saloon. Faro, the town drunkard, was studying it with the impersonal gravity of a somnolent owl. He glanced up at the man from Quirt, his eyes raking him slyly, the hostility carefully veiled. O'Rourke, out of the goodness of his heart and the softness of his head, had usually been good for at least one free drink a day. Now there were no free drinks to be had.

3

'So Long Rain is to acquire culture,' Faro murmured. 'The Great Lakes and Seaboard Players are to come among us—*after* showing their wares at New Cheyenne! Now that is something, that these old eyes should live to see the day or to behold when Selway's is crowded with a thirsty crew from Slash Y—denied their whiskey at O'Rourke's and refusing to patronize O'Dion's—but hungry, and on a Thursday!'

Having planted the barb, he shuffled away. Startled, Gordon glanced farther along the street, his eyes narrowing. It might be true, for this was a Thursday, and the hitch-rails on both sides of the street were lined with horses bearing the brand of Slash Y. The only horse with a Quirt brand was his own.

Quirt and Slash Y had been the big outfits in the valley of the Bitter Sage for almost as long as anyone could remember. Old Abe McKay had chosen the eastern section, then had built Slash Y to formidable proportions—a man who minded his own business and made certain that others did the same. Tom Landis had preempted the western half of the valley for his own at about the same time, making Quirt an equal power.

As long as Landis had run the Quirt, there had been no trouble. The rumblings of unrest had come when Curt O'Dion had arrived in the country, claiming Quirt as his own, explaining that he had bought it from Landis

4

when the latter had been on a trip to Chicago with a shipment of cattle. Landis had never returned to contradict him, and only one man had had the temerity to question O'Dion's account or claim to ownership. Boot Hill had acquired another tenant.

From that day, two years before, hostility between the two big outfits had increased, despite O'Dion's bland insistence that he wanted only good relations with all men.

Like most of Landis' crew, Brick Gordon had stayed on at Quirt. The pay was good, and O'Dion had quickly demonstrated that he knew the cattle business.

When trouble had threatened to erupt, it had been averted by a truce. Long Rain was trading headquarters for both outfits. Slash Y went to O'Rourke's Saloon, Quirt to The Silver Dollar. But at The Mercantile or at Selway's, the one good restaurant, trouble might erupt if they came together. So it had been agreed that Tuesdays, Thursdays, Saturdays, and the first and third Sundays of any month should be Quirt days in the town; the others were reserved for Slash Y. For more than a year, the truce had been observed.

But this was a Thursday, and Slash Y seemed to be in town in force. Which was hardly to be wondered at, with their saloon summarily closed and the rival liquor store owned by O'Dion. This show of resentment had probably been sparked by Driscoll McKay, the son of Abe, an ambitious man who was more and more taking over the running of the outfit.

From an impersonal point of view, Gordon could scarcely blame them; but he was a Quirt rider, and he felt a surge of annoyance, directed as much at his employer as at Slash Y. What the devil was O'Dion up to?

O'Dion knew that he'd been a good friend of the former owner; but they had gotten along well enough, at least until the last few weeks. Of late, there had been a subtle change in O'Dion's attitude toward him, shown in small but significant ways, such as sending him into town today, alone, on an errand which had turned out to be trivial. He was certain now that it had been merely an excuse.

Now he was in town, the sole representative of Quirt—and Quirt's crew were always expected to uphold the rather nebulous honor of Quirt.

O'Dion must have gotten wind of Slash Y's intention to show their contempt for the old agreement; but instead of meeting force with force, he'd sent Gordon in, alone. Why? He knew of Gordon's heady temper, and he knew what might happen to a man in such a situation. What was he up to?

Gordon pondered. He could ride out without his supper, but the word would run

6

at his heels that a Quirt man had been bluffed away from Selway's on a Quirt day. After such a show, or lack of it, he wouldn't be able to stay on at Quirt.

As far as staying was concerned, he wasn't at all sure that he cared to, the way things were going. On the other hand, as a Quirt man, also with his personal pride, he couldn't turn his back on a bluff. Besides, it was time to eat.

Gordon pushed open the door of Selway's and his irritation mounted as a survey confirmed his suspicion. All but one small table were occupied, and most of the customers belonged to Slash Y.

Looking around, he was conscious of the sudden silence. He'd been seen, and even those who didn't know him recognized him instinctively as belonging to Quirt. There was the flaming red hair, the casual look of gray eyes which seemed always to hold a hint of challenge.

A glance encountered his and locked briefly; blue eyes against gray, faintly mocking. The blue eyes belonged to Driscoll McKay. Gordon knew him as an aspiring man, resenting the fairly loose rein with which Abe had tethered him, greedy now to boss an outfit which he already looked upon as his.

He can't wait, Gordon thought, and found in that a clue to this invasion of the town on a

Thursday. 'Quirt's given him a good excuse—but he's looking for trouble and anxious to find it!'

He shrugged, feeling impatience and self-anger, then strode to the one table still unoccupied and drew out a chair. There would be no pleasure in eating there tonight, under the circumstances. There might well be trouble.

But he couldn't run, and in any case, he was hungry. And Selway's was the only restaurant worthy of the name.

A waiter came to take his order, eyes staring from a suddenly bloodless face. Disregarding his manifest nervousness, Gordon ordered.

'Steak and spuds, with tea.'

He caught the titter of amusement at the final item. Almost everybody drank coffee. Few had the temerity to order tea, even if they preferred it, among such a gathering. But he didn't care for Arbuckles, and he'd been having tea too long to quit now.

'Shut up, you fool! That's Gordon!'

The warning was a whisper; a man at the next table lost color, and the ripple of laughter subsided. Most men knew better than to laugh at Brick Gordon. Tonight he chose to ignore it. He was attacking his steak when he became aware of a newcomer hesitating at his table, and glanced up. It took an effort of will to forestall a sharp intake of

8

breath when he saw who stood there.

He'd seen Mary McKay two or three times since her return from the East, but always at a distance, never to speak to. On this or any other range, she was unforgettable. It was not that she was outstanding in figure or had any unusual combination of good looks. It was simply that she was Mary McKay, as he was Brick Gordon; and there was no one else quite like her.

Most women with yellow hair had hair merely yellow; Mary's was rich with the gold of autumn leaves, the richness extending to her cheeks. The effect was enhanced by the way her mouth turned up at the corners, the gleam in her eyes. The combination was arresting.

'Do you mind if I sit here?' She smiled, then took the other chair as he came to his feet.

'Happy to have you, ma'am.'

'Thank you.' She studied him carefully, clearly wondering who he was, noting the gesture, for not every man bothered to rise on such an occasion. 'I think I'll have the same as you,' she added. 'It looks good, even to the tea. I grow tired of coffee.'

'Coffee's fine in the morning,' he observed. 'Come evening, though, I like tea. Guess I must have some English in me somewhere.'

'That wouldn't be so bad, would it?' she asked, and to his surprise, Gordon found the conversation flowing along as though they had been old friends. He was aware that the rest of the room had more or less paused, watching, considering, as she took a seat at the table alongside a man from Quirt. But since she was the daughter of their boss, no one intervened. Even her brother, across the room contented himself with sharp watchfulness. Since her back was to him, Mary did not notice.

She was plainly unaware that she was eating and visiting with a Quirt rider, though Brick found himself wondering if she would care, even if she knew. From all reports, Mary McKay was an independent-minded young lady. She'd been away most of the three years that he'd worked for Quirt, attending an Eastern school. She had returned to Slash Y only a couple of months before.

Under the circumstances, he'd better ride a tight herd on himself and not allow himself any notions. Those would be easy, with so pretty a girl. But this was no time to be a fool.

Abruptly she leaned forward, smiling.

'We haven't even introduced ourselves,' she said. 'I'm Mary—Mary McKay.'

'I know, ma'am. And I'm pleased to meet you.'

A small frown appeared between her eyes.

'I said that I was "Mary," not "ma'am," she reminded him. 'And you haven't told me

10

your name.'

'I'm sorry, Mary. Folks call me Brick—Brick Gordon.'

'On account of your hair, of course. Anyhow, Brick, it fits.' Clearly she had not heard of him, or if so, did not recollect the name now. Again she leaned forward, a hint of mischief or challenge in her eyes.

'I'd like a glass of beer,' she observed, 'But they wouldn't bring it to me if I ordered it. Some folks are easily shocked. But you might do me a favor—by ordering it.'

He studied her a moment, his face expressionless, not bothering to tell her that he too was shocked at the request. Then he too began to feel reckless. The others would see—and they might be spurred to action. But if that was what she wanted—

'Whatever you wish,' he murmured, and signaled to the waiter, giving the order. A moment later, when a bottle and glass were brought, he filled the glass and shoved it across the table.

She smiled her thanks, then paused with the glass half to her lips. If she had done this to get action, she was not to be disappointed. At least a dozen chairs were scraping back, Slash Y men coming to their feet and converging on the small table like an avenging horde.

Driscoll McKay was not among them, but he was watching, plainly approving. Jim

11

Lomax, Slash Y foreman, acted as spokesman. He ignored his employer's daughter, and his voice rang harshly.

'Do you think you can get away with that, Gordon? We've put up with you eatin' at the same table with Miss McKay—but when you offer her liquor you go too far. Not the whole crew of Quirt could make that stick!'

Brick crouched tensely on the edge of his chair. His impulse was to heave to his feet, to face the bunch and outface or outfight them, but this was a time to keep a tight rein on his temper. The fact that they were there, on a day when only Quirt was supposed to have eating rights in the restaurant, rang as warningly as the shake of a diamondback's tail.

Was the girl in on the plot also? She had precipitated the trouble by her request, but the look on her face left him in doubt. She seemed to be astonished as well as dismayed at the reaction, and he was ready to withhold judgment where she was concerned.

Which was more than the others were in a mood to do with him. A hand fell heavily on his shoulder, fingers closing like claws. He tried to shake it off, and felt a jerk as another hand grabbed at his revolver and twitched it from the holster. His clutch for it was a fraction too slow; then, furious, he heaved to his feet, sending his chair crashing back with the violence of the motion.

The man who had grabbed his gun was spoiling for trouble. As a part of the same motion, he brought it up and aimed a smash of the blued steel barrel at Gordon's head, a rap which, had it landed as intended, would have dropped him like the bludgeon of an axe. He dodged, coming up under the blow, lashing out with bared knuckles, and his swing connected with the rim of a craggy jaw.

Long pent violence exploded in that swing, and the man who had appropriated his gun landed on his back in the middle of the adjoining table, his hair momentarily pillowed in a plate of gravy, spilling a cup of coffee over one of the occupants. His clutch on the six-gun loosened as he struck, allowing it to drop. Brick pounced and came up with it before any of the others could prevent him.

They were all around him. There was no chance to get his back to a wall, and the moment held the threat of unpleasantness. But there was a way to counter-attack. If you couldn't control a roomful, someone close at hand would do as well. He jabbed the muzzle of the gun into the ribs of Lomax, countering the foreman's move for his own gun.

'If anybody gets roughed up, Lomax, you top the list!' he warned.

The other man was getting off the wrecked table, feeling gingerly of his chin, shifting exploring fingers to the spot where the back of his head had come in contact with the

13

plate. Everyone in the room was now on his feet, half the men with hands on guns. Not until that moment had Gordon taken account of the fact all of them were armed. That was unusual, though not unknown, when Slash Y came to town.

'Make your choice,' he warned Lomax, and shoved with the gun point. 'Should I have to pull trigger, it would mean your death!'

It was the plight of Lomax that restrained the others. Apparently they had come to town on this particular day looking for trouble. But tempers had not yet outrun caution. Driscoll McKay shouldered forward.

'Easy, boys,' he warned. 'I'll handle this. Put up your guns, everybody.'

They hesitated, then obeyed as Lomax nodded confirmation. Shrugging, Gordon returned his own gun to its holster.

'The men are touchy about what you just did, Gordon,' Driscoll growled. 'Though you should have known better, Mary,' he added reprovingly. 'You were asking for trouble—'

Mary McKay had come to her feet with the rest, then stood, her eyes bright and watchful. Her face was faintly puzzled; there was clearly something in this which she did not understand. Now she tossed her head defiantly.

'I was asking for something for myself—and there was one gentleman in the room—only one,' she observed pointedly.

14

'Does it require all the rest of you, jumping like a pack of wolves, to deal with one?'

Blood coursed darkly under the skin of most of their faces at her question. Lomax attempted to answer.

'What made us mad was havin' a Quirt rider cozyin' up to you, Miss Mary. And when he tried to get you drunk—'

'Are you from Quirt?' Her attention returned to Gordon, her interest quickening. 'I didn't know that. As for the rest—' Her glance, blazing now like sun sweeping from behind a cloud, scorched Lomax, then came to rest on her brother. 'Are you a McKay, or even a man, to permit such insinuations to be cast? I came to his table, not he to mine—'

Driscoll managed a shrug. His voice was heavy.

'Now, sis, let's not indulge in a public airing of differences,' he suggested. 'There's fault on both sides.' His heavy-lidded stare fixed on Gordon. 'Only get one thing straight, Gordon, for your own good. Just because my sister made a mistake—don't go getting any notions where she's concerned!'

CHAPTER TWO

Riding home in the settling night, Gordon strove to sort out his emotions and impressions, and found both curiously tangled. Agreeing with Driscoll McKay on one point, he had clamped his jaw on the flood of words eager to spill off his tongue, turned in silence and walked out of the restaurant. Since a lady was involved, it was neither the time nor place for a public airing of differences.

And, in spite of her request for a drink, he was convinced that Mary McKay was a lady.

He was angry as well as confused, his anger directed chiefly at Slash Y for invading the town and restaurant on a day reserved for Quirt, at their arrogance and eagerness to stir up trouble. Still, Quirt had given plenty of provocation. In their place he would have done the same.

Apparently it had been partly chance, and partly the fact that there was no other place to sit, which had brought Mary McKay to his table. She had taken it for granted that he was one of the Slash crew.

Unwittingly, she had gotten him into trouble. But by the same token, she had gotten him out again. Except for the restraint imposed by her presence, he'd certainly have been involved in trouble from the moment he entered the restaurant.

Actually, he knew little concerning Mary McKay, scarcely more than she seemed to know about him. Along with Driscoll, she was heir to Slash Y, and it might not be long

16

before they would be coming into their inheritance. Thinking back, Brick realized it had been quite a while since he'd seen old Abe McKay, either in town or riding his range. Abe was getting old, and he kept increasingly close to his fireside. Between them, Driscoll and Lomax had been taking over the running of the ranch, deciding policy. Today's trip to town was almost certainly Driscoll's decision.

Mary was a relative newcomer in the situation, after being away for some years. Yet he couldn't understand how a girl raised on the range could lose touch with reality as completely as she seemed to have done. She had acted like a tenderfoot, to whom everything was strange.

His face burned as he recalled Driscoll's warning not to get any notions where she was concerned! The brass of the man! Did they think he was a fortune-hunter, or interested in anything connected with Slash Y, even its women?

Well, they could go to the devil, he told himself violently, all of them—then found himself amending that in his mind. Actually, it appeared as though Mary had been challenging the rest of them, being deliberately provocative in asking him to order the drink for her.

He hadn't approved, any more than they had, for a man didn't like to see a woman indulge in liquor—not her kind of a woman, at least. Even so, there was something about her which he admired, the flash of spirit, as well as the way she had condemned the rest of them sweepingly and scathingly.

He had taken note that her cheeks had bloomed scarlet when Driscoll had made that last biting remark about him not getting any notions.

To the devil with them—also with Quirt. He wouldn't run from trouble, not if it was legitimate. But what was brewing in the valley of the Bitter Sage threatened to be bitter indeed, and not at all to his liking. He was fed up. In the morning, he'd ride out and leave them to stew in their own juice.

Even though his decision was made, he was still seething when he unsaddled. Mary he could pardon on various grounds—either of ignorance, or the age-old excuse that she was a beautiful woman. But the men—

The buildings of Quirt were set in a secluded meadow among the hills. O'Dion's big house stood dark, looming monstrous by comparison with the other buildings, even the barn. A crew had worked nearly two years to build the house, hauling stone, erecting a massive dwelling which looked almost like a medieval castle. It seemed incongruous for an unmarried man who had spent the first three decades of his life in soddies or long shacks, when not curled up in a blanket on the open

18

range. But the house was O'Dion's, a symbol of the power for which he was hungrily on the reach.

The old bunk house, standing in the shadow of the bigger one, was alight and crowded. Gordon tried to slip in unobtrusively, but heads turned at his entrance, and even a poker face was not enough. They read something of his anger in the glint of his eyes, and clamored to know what had happened.

'A little trouble,' he admitted. 'When I went into Selway's for supper, it was crowded—with Slash Y riders.'

That stirred them. The fact that Quirt had been increasingly provocative made no difference. Slash Y had taken up the challenge and flung it back in their faces.

'What happened?' Felix Yankus asked the question. He usually spoke for Quirt, unless O'Dion was present.

'We had a few words.' Gordon shrugged. 'Nothing serious.'

'I'll bet!' One man laughed shortly.

Knowing Gordon's temper, the others too seemed to accept his disclaimer with reservations. But he had no intention of giving a full account, which would involve dragging in the name of Mary McKay. They discussed this move on the part of the Slash, and its possible implications, then went to bed.

They were finishing breakfast the next morning before Curt O'Dion entered the room and slid into his accustomed place. He was slight of figure for the power which he represented on the range, so that the big gun at his hip had the aspect of a burden. There was a flaunting twist to his mustache, and his voice could boom like a bellows.

His eyes swept the table in a quick survey, pausing an instant on Gordon, turning speculative. Whatever his thoughts, he gave no inkling of them.

'Take your time and keep your seats, boys. I've a word for everyone before you go.'

He helped himself characteristically to flapjacks, simply upending the platter which held a stack of a dozen onto his plate, sloshing syrup over the pile, and spearing a steak at the same time. He ate rapidly, with huge appetite, and it occurred to Gordon, remembering the darkened big house, that he looked like a man who might have spent the night riding rather than sleeping.

No one questioned him. On Quirt, men had long since learned not to show surprise when O'Dion gave an order.

He shoved his empty plate away, drained a third cup of coffee, and leaned back with a gusty sigh of satisfaction. For a second time his glance fixed speculatively on Gordon, and it was clear that he had been told what had taken place in town. But he made no direct reference to that when he spoke.

'There is in the Good Book a place where the Man of Wisdom speaks. He proclaims that there is a time for everything—a time to be sad, a time to be merry, a time to be born, a time to die. Everything in its proper time and place. No wonder he was called wise.'

No one answered. To them, it did not appear incongruous that O'Dion should quote from the Good Book. They had heard him do it too often.

'So it is that I've been biding my time, waiting for the right time. And now it has arrived. The natives are restless.' He smiled, a tight grin which held no humor. 'As you know, Slash has been getting notions. Yesterday they chose to break the truce. That was their doing, not ours, and such vain glory on their part must be curbed. Also, it is time for Quirt to expand, and now they have given us the signal to move ahead. Therefore we shall gird up our loins and take possession of the land.'

Expectancy showed on every face, but no one interrupted.

O'Dion's voice took on the purring quality of a puma. He leaned forward, arms on the table. With the sleeves rolled above his elbows, they were revealed to be as hairy as his upper lip.

'Your duties will include more riding, and there will be some branding to do—even the

21

altering of brands, if those already on the hide show wrong. It is my intention that one brand shall become predominant on this range. And that brand is Quirt.'

There were quick intakes of breath as his meaning became clear. This was a declaration of war, an assertion that the Slash must be driven from the range. To men who knew O'Dion, the pronouncement was not surprising. He had grown accustomed to having his own way, and those who got in it were apt to be stepped on.

'There may be some trouble,' he added. 'But I don't think that will worry any of us. The warrior sniffs the battle from afar and glories in it. I tell you, so that you will be ready. One other thing. The laborer is worthy of his hire. As Quirt profits, so will you who ride for Quirt.'

Heads nodded with satisfaction. This was O'Dion's way of replying to the insult and challenge offered Quirt the evening before. Slash had asked for war, so war it would be, to the finish.

No one doubted O'Dion's assurance that they should share in the rewards. He asked a lot of his men when occasion demanded, but he was never niggardly in paying them. The trouble was that the bonus always came from someone else's till, as when he'd gotten the idea of turning O'Rourke's Saloon into an opera house.

Moments before, he'd forced O'Rourke to accept a niggardly five hundred dollars in cash for his building and business. Then, smiling blandly, he'd emptied O'Rourke's till of more than a thousand dollars, announcing that the money would be O'Rourke's contribution to the new enterprise, to pay the costs of alteration.

Someone would be expected to pay for this now. Slash Y, perhaps. Certainly someone other than Curt O'Dion. His open-handedness never extended to his own pocketbook.

O'Dion paused, eying his crew, and seemed satisfied. This was a rough, tough crew; all others had been weeded out, and replacements were handier with guns than with the tools of a cowboy's trade. He'd been getting ready for this ever since he had acquired Quirt.

'Be ready for anything,' O'Dion added, 'starting today.'

Some started to shove back from the table. Gordon's voice halted the exodus.

'In that case, O'Dion, I'll be taking my time now,' he observed.

The others looked at him in surprise, almost with shock. For anyone to question the boss at such a moment was unusual, but that the rebel should be Brick Gordon was doubly so, particularly after what had happened the day before.

Curt O'Dion was a hard man, and proud of his reputation. He had long boasted that he kept a tough crew of fighting men, and it was universally accepted that Brick Gordon was the toughest of the hardcase crew. Not that he went about looking for trouble, as some of them did, or provoked it unduly. But when it came, no one had a better capacity for dealing with it.

O'Dion's gaze swiveled to him, and again there was a speculative expression in the back of his eyes. There was something here beyond his understanding, and that bothered Gordon.

'Your time, did you say, Brick?' O'Dion put the purr back in his voice, but the claws of the cat scratched through. 'Was it that which you said, or were my ears playin' me tricks?'

Gordon shrugged.

'Your ears are good enough. I'll have my time.'

'But I don't understand. You wouldn't want to quit when there's trouble on the wind, a bit of thunder to the west. Not when the war horse sniffs the battle from afar—'

'This horse doesn't like the smell,' Gordon retorted bluntly. 'So I'm quitting.'

'The devil you are! After what happened last night, I'd think you'd relish the chance to get back at the Slash.'

'I might, at that. But when it comes to

going outside the law, count me out.'

O'Dion's color matched the hair on Gordon's head. Not even his foreman had ever had the temerity to talk to the boss of Quirt in such a fashion.

'You are saying that you do not approve of the methods which I have outlined?'

'Whether I approve or not is beside the point. I don't care to be a part of such a deal. That's all.'

'Oh, and that is all, is it now? It appears that we have one righteous man in the congregation of the sinful—behold him! And should we crawl on our knees and change our ways on that account?'

There was something here which went far beyond the surface, an acrimony, almost a personal hatred which were new in Gordon's relations with his employer. What was happening now was being used by O'Dion as an excuse; it was not the cause. Well, whatever his reason or motive, to the devil with him.

'I'm not asking you to change your ways or telling you what to do. I'm merely taking my time.'

'The man is taking his time, he says—and riding out, after what I have revealed of our plans—doing so frankly because I supposed myself surrounded by a loyal crew of trustworthy men. But of course it's not that easy nor simple.'

'Do you think I'd run to Slash Y and tell them what you have in mind?' Gordon's temper was also rising.

'A man who would quit at such a time just might play the part of a Judas,' O'Dion returned grimly. Triumph threaded his tone, as though in spite of his disclaimer, the turn of events was to his liking. 'On that score we take no chances. No one quits at this juncture—least of all you.'

Gordon felt a mild astonishment at himself. Certainly he had been seething at the treatment accorded him by Slash, and here was a perfect opportunity to get back at them. Only the evening before he had been one man against an entire crew, and had come dangerously close to being manhandled. Now he was taking a stand against a crew of equal size, and as lacking in squeamishness. And for what?

Certainly not from any love for Slash Y. He'd always given a grudging respect to old Abe McKay, who was a hard man but fair. He was also tough, as a man had to be to hold his own on such a range, particularly when confronted by an outfit such as Quirt had become under O'Dion.

As for the rest of Slash Y, they were competent men who did their job, and were ready to fight, if need be, at the drop of a hat.

At the top now was Driscoll McKay, backed by Jim Lomax, spoiling for trouble, apparently as eager as Quirt. Driscoll he considered more a fool than a leader, even though Driscoll had restrained his crew the evening before. Perhaps he'd done so out of consideration for his sister, though more like it had been because he'd realized that Lomax would be the first to suffer.

Certainly Brick had no reason for gratitude, either to Driscoll McKay or his outfit. Nor was he doing it for Mary McKay—who, whatever her intention might have been, had gotten him into a bad fix and all but made a fool of him. He wasn't concerned with her one way or another—and never would be, he reminded himself angrily.

If he took his time and rode out now, he'd keep going on to some distant range. The plain truth was that he drew the line at rustling, at blotting of brands.

'I'll overlook what you're suggesting, O'Dion,' he returned. 'But I'm taking my time—now. This is a free country, and I'm a free man—and don't forget it!'

This time there could be no doubt. The flicker of triumph in O'Dion's eyes could not be hidden. Gambler though he might be, he was no poker player, and all disclaimers to the contrary, he was pleased at the turn events had taken.

CHAPTER THREE

Only a double-barreled chump, Gordon reflected bitterly, would fail to learn a lesson the first time. In town, the evening before, he had allowed them to get the jump on him; in part, that had happened because there was a lady present, and he, in a sense, had been her host. In addition, he hadn't supposed that Slash Y was so eager for trouble as to send their whole crew against one man.

The fact remained that they'd sneaked his gun and had had him at a disadvantage—and he should have profited by that lesson.

Yet now, for a second time, he'd been caught off guard, not supposing that the men who had been his trail mates for years would turn so suddenly and savagely. Mitch Noland worked the trick, lunging in from the side, slamming shoulder and arm into Gordon's ribs, throwing him against the man on the other side. While he was off balance, Yankus pinned his arms; then it seemed that the whole crew were swarming over him like ants on a strayed beetle.

One took his gun. He fought back, but the odds were too great. They twisted his arms behind his back, and Yankus drove a jarring fist into the middle of his stomach. The blow was so savage that it left him gasping and breathless. While he was helpless, it seemed that every man sought to hit him at least once, as though by such a show to court the approval of O'Dion.

The boss watched with no change of expression, speaking no word of restraint. It was Mitch Noland, eying with sudden revulsion the blood on his fist, blood not his own, who cried out in protest and shoved his own considerable bulk as a shield, grabbing two men who still came on and holding them, struggling but helpless.

'That's enough,' he said thickly. 'What are we—wolves? After all, he's one of us.'

Gordon was still on his feet, held by a man on either side. The red haze was not due to his own anger.

'You're right, Mitch,' O'Dion murmured. 'He's had a lesson—perhaps enough of one. Maybe our ears were deceivin' us, Brick. Could it be that we didn't hear quite right? Are you going along with the rest of us?'

It wasn't often that O'Dion gave any man a second chance. For him, it was a big concession. Gordon's face was a bloody smear, the agony of the savage attack still rocking through him. He spat defiance.

'This is the sort of thing I expected from Slash,' he returned: 'a whole crew jumping one man! Now I'd sooner work with the devil!'

Yankus moved threateningly, but Noland

raised a big paw, and O'Dion continued to regard Brick almost sorrowfully.

'Some are slow to learn,' he observed. 'Having eyes, they can't see the shape of things to come, and their ears are plugged.' He tugged at an end of his mustache, his facial muscles twitching in sympathy with the jerk. 'Perhaps he needs a bit of cooling off, a chance to think the matter over. Let it not be said of us at Quirt that we are lacking in patience.'

An answering gleam flickered in the eyes of Yankus.

'Maybe the bear pit would be a good place for thinking,' he suggested.

O'Dion regarded his foreman with approval.

'What could be better?' he agreed. 'A quiet place—a secret place. When you are ready to come out, on our side again, you have but to say the word, Brick.'

'And if I don't choose to come crawling?'

'There will be no crawling required.' A second time the mustache jerked. 'But it runs in my mind that perhaps we have been careless in leaving such an open pit—that maybe it should be filled in again—like a grave.'

With the threat ringing in his ears, they dragged Gordon away, and he knew O'Dion well enough to be sure that he had heard his doom pronounced, unless he changed his mind. The bear pit was a mile from the buildings, a yawning hole in the middle of a tiny meadow, among a scraggly growth of jack pine. The irony, which would not go unappreciated by O'Dion, was that Gordon had been the one to suggest the pit in the first place.

It had come about because Quirt had been suffering depredations over a long period at the paws of a renegade grizzly. The bear had been dubbed The Beef Eater, because of his fondness for cattle. His toll was an average of one cow or steer each week, and he had a disconcerting habit of striking at widely separated points, often miles apart. Efforts to shoot or trap the bear had failed.

Gordon had made the discovery that on several occasions the big grizzly had followed the same trail, venturing close to the buildings of Quirt, as though taking a close look at the situation. One bull had been killed in the corrals.

Other methods having failed, Gordon had pointed out that a pit, dug where the trail crossed the open meadow, then carefully covered over, might bring the cow killer to destruction. The pit had been dug, sheer-walled and deep, roofed and left in place.

On the very next morning, going for a look, they had approached with high hopes, noting that the roof had collapsed, that something was certainly trapped in the pit. Then elation had given way to disgust, as they found at the bottom a deer with a broken neck. The sign around the brink of the hole had offered mute testimony that now the grizzly would never be taken in it.

Claw marks were all around the rim, obviously from the twisted foot of the bear, injured in a trap years before. Apparently The Beef Eater had been approaching, exactly as hoped; a deer had fled before him, falling into the pit, and the grizzly had examined the trap in detail. Knowing of its existence, he would not be fooled by it.

In one sense the pit might be said to have worked, for oddly enough, the depredations had stopped. Whether the killer had taken the hint and left the country, or been overtaken by misfortune in the wilds, there had been no more sign of him. A wire fence had been built around the pit to keep cattle from falling in, and it had gone almost forgotten.

Dragged along by a man clutching either arm, Gordon was dumped unceremoniously into the hole. If he, like the deer, suffered a broken neck, they were in no mood to care. By the time he picked himself up, shaken but no worse than bruised, only the receding sounds of footsteps came to his ears.

A look around his prison was not reassuring. It was twenty feet deep and a dozen feet across. Weather and water had caused little erosion of the walls, and while some debris had fallen in, not enough had collected to afford any foundation from which to climb. A few attempts to escape convinced him of what he had known: that it was impossible. Once, working desperately, he made it to within half a dozen feet of the rim, only to have an outjut of soil and rock break loose and pitch him back. That time he landed hard and lay breathess.

The day dragged. Flies came to keep him company, attracted by the dry blood on his face, a constant irritation. There was plenty of time for reflection, to wonder if anger and pride were to be his undoing. He could still change his mind and work with the rest of Quirt's crew; he had no doubt that O'Dion would succeed. Old Abe McKay no longer bulked formidably in the way of his ambitions, and Gordon, like O'Dion, doubted that Driscoll McKay would prove much of an adversary.

They'd simply bleed the Slash, as a weasel sucks the blood of a victim, until it could struggle no more. Other small outfits could be counted on to stand aloof from such a struggle. Their own eventual salvation might lie in combining now to fight alongside the Slash, but for many reasons they would not. By the time they woke up to their danger, it would be too late.

The only other possible deterrent was the law, and O'Dion had made sure that he would have nothing to fear from that. The sheriff and the judge owed their election and their allegiance to O'Dion. Any gesture they made to stop him would be no more than a token one.

You have a chance to be in on the winning side—or to stay in this hole forever, Gordon reminded himself. And a sensible man would swallow his pride!

The trouble was that he was not sensible. He'd had his doubts about the deal by which O'Dion had acquired Quirt, and those had increased with O'Dion's subsequent activities. But he was a cowhand, and so long as he was called upon to do no more than a cowboy's proper work, he'd done so, though with increasing watchfulness.

Now O'Dion was demanding brand blotching and wholesale thievery, and that was something else. Also, there was O'Dion's inexplicable attitude toward himself, recent in origin but unmistakable. It was as though O'Dion were anxious to be rid of him, but not by allowing him to quit or go as a free agent.

That Mary McKay and her heritage were involved in this, he told himself angrily, made no difference.

It was evening before anyone came near. He heard the sound of footsteps, a single man, the creak of the barbed wire fence as the strands were parted to allow passage between. He was not surprised that it was Felix Yankus who gazed down at him, his heavy face gloating and resentful. In his foreman O'Dion had found a kindred spirit, though Yankus lacked the surface polish of his boss.

The foreman held a tray in both hands, and Gordon made out that it was laden with food and something to drink. Thirst had become a torture during the long afternoon.

'You have enough, Brick?' Yankus asked. 'I've brought you some supper—if you're ready for it. And then you can come along back.'

'Throw me a rope or something, then,' Gordon replied.

Yankus set the tray down, then scowled suspiciously.

'You ready to go along and do as the boss says?' he demanded.

'Let's talk after I've eaten,' Gordon suggested, but Yankus was not so easily fooled. He shook his head, grinning crookedly.

'No, sir. You give your word first, or you stay right there. And it can get to be uncomfortable, fillin' your belly on air. Make it quick, or I'm going to eat this grub. I just had a good feed, but I can enjoy another.'

Deliberately, sitting down, he started to eat. He was obviously enjoying it, drinking noisily, and Gordon was forced to watch helplessly. They would take his word, because they knew that once he gave it, he'd stick to a promise. Short of that, O'Dion would abide by his threat, leaving him to die by slow degrees. O'Dion, of course, was sure that he wouldn't be so foolish as to hold out very long.

Yankus sighed gustily, wiping his mouth with the back of a hand, pushing the tray to one side. He got slowly to his feet.

'That was good grub,' he observed, and proceeded to enumerate the bill of fare, from fried chicken to biscuits to apple pie, each item mouth-watering to his auditor. 'Might be the cook could find some more for you back at the cook house. 'Course, if you ain't interested—'

'How does it feel to be a worm, Yankus?' Brick asked. 'And so low that you could crawl under a rattlesnake without it knowing? Or are you so much a worm that you don't even know the difference?'

Night was beginning to settle, filling the little meadow among the trees with dusk, but enough light remained to reveal the dark flush on the foreman's face. His voice choked with rage.

'Who you callin' a worm?' he demanded. 'Why, blast you, I'm just doing what I was told—'

'Sure you are,' Gordon cut in. 'That's all you know, to do as you're told. That's what

36

slaves do. You couldn't think for yourself if you tried, or even act like a man. You're the sort who hits a man when he can't fight back, a gully-whuzzler that even a coyote would turn up his nose at!'

Yankus looked momentarily puzzled.

'I ain't nothin' of the sort,' he protested. 'What's a gully-whuzzler?'

'You are,' Gordon retorted. 'The lowest crawlin' form of gully-whuzzler.'

He'd made up the term on the spur of the moment. As he'd expected, it enraged the slow-thinking Yankus simply because he didn't understand it. He glared wildly around, frustrated by the distance between them, then darted from sight for a moment, returning almost at once with a long, slender pole. Gordon had noticed it that morning, when his captors had dragged him to the prison.

Originally, many saplings had been cut and trimmed and used to bridge the pit, with grass and leaves fashioned above to conceal the trap. Most of those had disappeared in the year and more since the pit was built, but a few remained. He taunted Yankus in the hope of enraging him.

Now, torn between rage and wild glee, Yankus leaned forward, reaching down, thrusting with one end of the pole, trying to prod or hit him. A wild swing almost succeeded, but Gordon jumped aside.

'See what I mean?' he shouted. 'A gully-whuzzler!'

Yankus raced halfway around the rim, surprisingly agile for so big a man, and took another swing. Deliberately, Gordon sprawled and lay as though he'd been hurt. Yankus chortled triumphantly and thrust viciously with the pole. Twisting, Gordon grabbed the end, and before Yankus could understand the trick, gave a savage jerk in return. If he could get possession of the pole, he'd have a tool to aid him in climbing from the pit. But what happened was even better.

Yankus was clutching his end of the pole doggedly and, taken off-guard, he came along with it, losing his balance and toppling. He landed heavily, then lay prone. A quick examination convinced Gordon that the wind was merely knocked out of him, but that was enough.

Setting the pole upright at the edge, using it both for balance and climbing, he was at the top by the time Yankus was able to sit up and take a renewed interest in affairs. Tossing the pole aside, Gordon looked down. By now it was virtually dark at the bottom of the hole.

'Somebody will probably help you out tomorrow,' he said, then snapped his fingers in exasperation. He'd been in so big a hurry to get out before Yankus recovered that he'd forgotten to help himself to Yankus' gun. Now it was too late.

A bullet came so close that he heard it sing past his ear. He jumped back, then moved away. The shooting would be heard, and others would come on the run. Still worse, once the crew was alerted, he couldn't very well return to the buildings, either to get his horse or to help himself to some grub.

CHAPTER FOUR

Disgusted, Brick set off. At least he was free of the pit, and the settling night was in his favor. Curt O'Dion was a realist, so he probably wouldn't bother with much of a hunt, knowing how hopeless the effort would be.

On the other hand, if he remained in that country, O'Dion and the crew of Quirt would be relentless and unforgiving. Something had prompted O'Dion to send him into the town the day before, knowing that he'd probably run into trouble. Now, in the face of his defiance, O'Dion would be angry and apprehensive, because he'd expect him to go to the Slash, tell what he knew and offer his services.

It would be logical, according to O'Dion's way of thinking, first to get back at Quirt, secondly to be near Mary McKay. His meeting with her the evening before would

39

loom in O'Dion's mind as the primary reason for Gordon's course of conduct. He'd probably assume that there was more to it than had actually been the case.

The thought brought Gordon up short. Certainly he didn't like the Slash or anything connected with the outfit—for even Mary, whether wittingly or not, had contrived to make a fool of him. Yet now Curt O'Dion's rage would be aimed at her as well as at himself, as he linked the two in his mind. That being so, did he have any right to pull out now and head for a new range, leaving Mary to face such a predicament?

It was easy to tell himself that none of this was his quarrel, that it would be the part of wisdom to go fast and far, leaving all of them to stew in the juice of their own brewing. The trouble was that Quirt had made it his fight, whether he liked it or not. And he'd never made a practice of running from a fight.

Nonetheless, a lot of pros were involved, as well as cons. The question was still unresolved in his mind when he heard the faint jingle of a bridle bit and saw the shadowy outline of a horse, cropping the grass. A faint hump above its back confirmed the rest; it was a saddle horse, with reins dragging, and certainly miles from where it should have been.

That might mean that its rider had been thrown and was somewhere nearby, perhaps injured and helpless. Or the horse could belong to a rider from Quirt, posted to watch for him. He hadn't expected O'Dion to go that far, but it was a possibility.

He was some five miles from the buildings on Quirt, and by the same token about an equal distance from the headquarters of the Slash. This was Quirt range, but it wasn't far to the line between the two outfits.

The moon, nearly at the full tonight, would be up soon. Its glow was already spreading across the east. He could detect nothing suspicious, and a horse was what he stood most in need of. Not of a mind to blunder into another trap, he moved cautiously. He'd slaked his thirst at a small tributary of the Bitter Sage, but the memory of the long day remained vivid.

At his approach, the horse raised its head, but did not try to shy away. True to its training, it stood ground-hitched when the reins were dropped, though hunger had caused it to graze, moving about. That indicated that it had been there for some time. A look at its left flank confirmed his guess. The brand was the Slash Y.

Imprisoned as he had been through the day, he had no knowledge of what might have happened. There could have been a clash between the two outfits. He'd have a look before going on.

Moving in a widening circle, he soon found

what he had feared. Half-hidden among grass and brush was the sprawled figure of a man. The sudden glow of the moon, rolling across the horizon, helped pick it out.

His first guess was that the man was dead, probably for some hours. Then, bending over and placing a hand on a shoulder, he decided that the fellow was still alive. At least he was warm, not rigid, though he lay face down in the grass. Turning him for a look, Gordon started back in shock.

It was Driscoll McKay.

The moonlight showed a face drained of blood, almost marble-white. But there was blood lower down, under an armpit—blood half-dry, yet still sticky. The wound did not look particularly ugly, being only a small hole which had not bled too much. That, he knew, was only the outward and superficial aspect.

It had been made by a bullet, which had gone in and was still embedded somewhere within his body. That in itself was apt to be bad. The lack of bleeding in this instance could not be considered reassuring. McKay was unconscious, and judging by the signs, he had been lying so for hours.

There was only one thing to do, and that was to get him on his horse and back to Slash Y, and then, if he was still alive, to send for a doctor. Moving him could be bad, but to leave him would mean certain death. One alternate was almost as grim as the other.

Driscoll's gun was not in his holster, and a brief search near the body failed to discover it. There was no time for a thorough hunt, even though a gun in his own pocket would have been comfortable insurance at this juncture. Gordon brought up the horse.

It was the manner in which the cayuse lifted its head, ears cocked forward, which warned that others were approaching. By then, with the moonlight flooding the landscape, there was not time to slip away, no chance to hide. Half a dozen horsemen came suddenly into sight, cresting the slope above, then came on at a brisk trot. The glint of the moon shone on drawn guns.

They surrounded him, exclaiming, suddenly angry as they recognized him, then made out the recumbent form of Driscoll McKay. The six were from the Slash, Jim Lomax at their head.

Lomax bent above McKay, then straightened grimly.

'What you got to say for yourself, Gordon?' he demanded.

'I came upon him a little while ago,' Gordon explained. 'I was just getting ready to load him onto his horse, to take him to his home.'

'That's a likely story,' one of the others exclaimed hotly. 'You shot him, and we caught you dead to rights. Why don't we string him up for the murderin' killer he is?'

Lomax lifted a restraining hand. His eyes remained fixed on Gordon's face.

'You and he didn't get on very well together the last time you met,' he reminded Brick.

'True enough,' Gordon conceded. 'But use your head. He's been here for hours—his horse had done a lot of grazing. That wound is far from fresh. I've no horse—and no gun.'

Lomax had reason to feel distrust and hostility, but he hadn't been made foreman at the Slash without possessing qualities of leadership. He nodded grudgingly.

'Go on.'

'That's it. I found him, after sighting his horse. I figured the best thing was to get him to Slash Y. It would be risky, but to leave him would be worse.'

There was another grudging nod. 'If you didn't shoot him, then who did?'

'I could make a guess, but you can do that as well as I can. Quirt is on the war path against the Slash. That's not news to you. For the rest—' He shrugged.

Lomax made a decision. 'Load him onto his horse,' he instructed. 'Gently, now. We've got to take him in. You'll come along, Gordon.'

'Suits me,' Gordon agreed. 'When he's able to talk, he'll tell you what happened, which will clear me.'

'It had better—and you'd better hope that

he's able to talk again,' Lomax grunted. 'Otherwise I wouldn't want to be in your boots.'

'You say you found him this way. But what the blazes are you doing here, that you found him?' another man burst out impatiently. 'And on foot, without a gun?'

'Since you ask, I'm runnin' from Quirt,' Gordon returned, 'minus both those articles. All at once we didn't see eye to eye.'

'You tryin' to tell us that you've quit and they're after you?' The other man snorted derisively. 'You better make up a better story than that, or come daylight, we'll be decoratin' a tree.'

Gordon did not bother to reply. A quick search seemed to confirm his claim that he was on foot, and, grudgingly, he was given a seat behind Sam Drake, a thoughtful man who had remained in the background at the restaurant the evening before.

They made their way back to the Slash, taking their time, since haste would be hard on the injured man. McKay remained unstirring, and Gordon's anxiety was reflected on the faces of the others. Lomax dispatched a couple of the crew, one to ride straight for a doctor, the other to get a wagon and return, meeting them along the way.

Most of the ride had been completed before the wagon met them, with blankets spread over straw in the box. The transfer was made,

45

still with no visible change in the wounded man.

The ranch buildings came into sight, with lights everywhere, and there was a bustle of preparation. Mary McKay came hurrying to meet them, pale with dread. Looking up, her eyes widened as they met Gordon's, then mirrored both surprise and apprehension.

'You!' The word was so hushed that he could barely hear. 'What are you doing here?'

Lomax answered for him.

'We found him 'side of your brother, Mary. Gordon claims he'd just found him—but we'd like some more explainin' about that.'

'But I don't understand.' Suddenly she did, and indignation replaced the perplexity on her face. 'You don't mean that you think he might have done it?' she protested. 'Oh, no! He's not that sort.'

Gordon eased off the horse from behind Drake and managed a bow.

'I'm obliged for your good opinion, Miss McKay,' he said. 'As I pointed out to the others, your brother had been shot quite a while before I found him. Besides, I've no gun.'

'He claims that he's quit Quirt—and that they're after him,' Lomax added. 'That's harder to swallow than the rest.'

'You men!' Mary exclaimed impatiently. As though despairing of male stupidity, she

46

climbed on to the brake hub of the wagon and peered down at her brother, studying him anxiously. 'Get a door to move him on,' she instructed, and watched while Driscoll was lifted from the wagon and carried into the house. Catching sight of a loitering figure in the shadows of the big porch, she hurried to him.

'It's Driscoll, Pa,' she explained. 'He's been shot—badly hurt. They've just brought him in.'

Abe McKay asked no questions as to why he had not been informed sooner. Probably they had supposed him to be asleep. His voice seemed devoid of emotion.

'How bad?'

'We don't know,' Mary confessed. 'The wound looks pretty mean. We've sent for the doctor.'

'He's still alive, then?'

'Yes.'

'Tell me about it.'

Lomax had moved alongside Gordon. 'Stick around,' he said gruffly.

'I'm as interested in this as you are,' Gordon reminded him.

Lomax supplied such details as he knew, including the account of how they had come upon Gordon. McKay stood, his back to the side of the house, his face hidden in the shadows. If any of the things he was told surprised him, he gave no sign.

47

'Better have a look at his wound,' he observed, 'see if there's anything you can do. Most likely be hours before the doc can get here. You have a look, Gordon,' he added. 'From what I hear, you've had experience with gunshot wounds.'

It was true, and Gordon had taken charge on more than one occasion when there were injuries at Quirt, before the doctor could come. What surprised him was that McKay should know about this.

He helped Mary wash and cleanse the wound as well as possible. Since the bleeding had stopped, there was not much else to do. Lomax suggested getting some whiskey between Driscoll's lips as a stimulant, but McKay, from the background, promptly vetoed that.

'No whiskey. Better to leave him as he is, if he's restin' easy. You agree, Gordon?'

Surprised at having his opinion sought, Gordon nodded. 'Yes. To revive him now might kill him, once the effect of the stimulant wore off. Only a doctor can probe for that bullet, for it's uncomfortably close to his heart.'

'My opinion, too.' McKay nodded. 'Keep a good watch on him, in case he shows signs of waking up. Better put on the coffeepot. Now what's this, Gordon, about O'Dion's plan concerning Quirt?'

'From what he told us yesterday, I gather

that he is out to take over this whole range. He's been building toward that ever since he came, and now he thinks the time is ripe.'

'Yeah, there's been plenty of sign along the way. Now he's coming into the open—and shooting from ambush?'

'This shooting has all the earmarks. He intends to blot brands, whatever is necessary to smash the Slash.'

'In other words, war?'

'He knows it'll come to that.'

'And so you quit, rather than go along?'

'Yes.'

Abe nodded, as though not surprised. Mary came with coffee, one of the crew following with tin cups. Gordon downed his with relish, accepting a couple of refills. In the yellow light of the kerosene lamps, Mary's face appeared drawn and pale, but she was steady and efficient. No one thought of sleeping. Abe questioned the others about Driscoll's movements during the day, but no one had seen him ride away. Only when night had closed down and he had failed to return had alarm been felt. Some of them had set out to search.

Ordinarily, no one would have been concerned, but the trouble at Selway's the night before had made them uneasy.

Abe had listened quietly, but now his face showed sharp attention. He rapped a question.

'What's this about you bustin' in on Selway's last night? That was Thursday—and a Quirt night.'

Two or three of the crew exchanged startled, guilty glances. Clearly, they had betrayed something about which the boss had been in ignorance. Lomax sought to explain.

'Well, we were all in town yesterday, and it was time to eat. There didn't seem to be anybody from Quirt around, so we went to Selway's. We're tired of being pushed around by Quirt,' he added defensively.

'That was Driscoll's notion, I take it—about being tired of being pushed around and eatin' at Selway's?'

'Well—yes, I guess it was.'

'And somebody from Quirt *was* there?'

'Nobody to start with. Gordon came in while we were eating.'

'Gordon, eh? And then what?'

'There was some trouble.'

'I bet,' Abe said dryly. 'All of you against one. How much trouble?'

'Nothing to speak of. Not with Mary there—'

'Uh huh. And you and Driscoll didn't see fit to inform me of any of this. As foreman, you're workin' for Driscoll, eh, not me? I'm on the shelf, and what I say don't count any longer. That it, Mister?'

Lomax was sweating, acutely uncomfortable. He ran a finger around his shirt

50

collar as though it choked him.

'That's not so, Abe. It was just—just—'

'Just that you and Driscoll figured to take over here on Slash, and you needed a diversion to make it look right—trouble with Quirt. So you asked for trouble, and now you've got it. Somebody coming?'

The others heard it then, though Abe had been the first to catch the sound. A surrey wheeled into sight, drawn by a team of high-stepping bays. Doctor Porter, pudgy and graying at the temples, tossed the reins to one of the crew, then moved briskly to the house. He paused for a word with the McKays, then followed Mary.

Silence settled, almost as heavy as the surrounding blackness. It was nearly an hour before the doctor emerged, followed by Mary. Her face was composed, but her eyes were red.

'We tried,' Porter reported gruffly. 'It was a chance—but a slim one. And it didn't work. He's dead.'

CHAPTER FIVE

Now that the verdict had been given, Gordon realized that he had expected nothing else. The thread of hope had been as slender as a spider's web; there had been little chance that

51

Driscoll McKay might ever regain consciousness, to tell what he knew concerning who had struck him down—or who had not.

Angry mutterings arose from some of the men. Evidence or lack of it notwithstanding, it had been Brick Gordon whom they had caught at the scene of the murder.

'I say, let's string him up!' one rebel growled. 'He's Quirt, ain't he—and they're all guilty!'

The even, quiet voice of Abe McKay cut across the rising clamor like a slosh of cold water. He had returned, unnoticed, to loiter in the shadows. His face was strained and drawn, but he was still the boss.

'Quit such talk! Now, Lomax, what you got to say?'

Put suddenly on the spot, Lomax was caught off guard.

'Well, I don't quite know,' he admitted. 'But there's an old saying that seems to apply—an eye for an eye and a tooth for a tooth!'

Abe snorted derisively.

'Is that the best you can come up with? You're a fool,' he added bluntly, 'same as Driscoll was. I let him talk me into puttin' you in as foreman, though I knew it was a mistake. Not that it mattered too much, as long as I could look after things myself. Now it matters plenty. And there's no room for a

52

fool to head up things on Slash.'

Apparently the demotion was not unexpected, but Lomax listened incredulously as McKay continued.

'After what happened the night before in town, Driscoll should have known better than to ride alone, specially off on Quirt range. His trouble was that he never knew much—and he didn't live long enough to learn! So now we're in a mess.'

'Quirt can't get away with this,' Lomax protested thickly. 'We'll hit back at them.'

'They've gotten away with it,' McKay reminded him. 'Driscoll's dead. Nothing is going to change that. Sure we'll fight back—but doing it blind, striking senselessly, would finish us. That's what they're hoping we'll do; they're trying to goad us into riding into a trap. How do you figure it, Gordon?'

'I wouldn't be surprised if that was back of this shooting,' Gordon conceded. 'They aimed to be rid of the man they figured to be in charge, and driving Slash crazy mad at the same time.'

'Sure, that's bound to be the reason. O'Dion figures he's got us on the run and half licked already. And he might have been right, with a little luck. Only he made a mistake by not knowin' a man when he saw one. I can't handle this fight myself, and he's countin' on that. With Driscoll out of the way, O'Dion thought we would be finished. We might have been if he'd used some sense at home. But now that you're here, Gordon, will you take charge? I know it's askin' a lot—but a lot's at stake!'

Gordon had seen the request coming. Up to a few hours before, it would have seemed incredible, but he was beginning to understand how Abe McKay's mind worked. In a physical sense, Abe was all but helpless, but his mind was unimpaired. He could still go to the heart of a matter, brushing aside all trivialities.

The habit of command was strong, not readily broken. Lomax gave a yelp of protest.

'Are you crazy, McKay,' he demanded, 'askin' *him* to take over as foreman, and Driscoll not yet in his grave?'

'I'm still owner here,' McKay reminded him tartly. 'And what I say goes. As for Driscoll—maybe he's where he can see clearer now. Given time, he'd have gotten sense. But leavin' him out of it—*you* got any good reason why I shouldn't hire Gordon?'

'Plenty of them,' Lomax blazed. Resentment at his own demotion was inflamed by what seemed to him the monstrous choice of a man from Quirt.

'He'll be here—right along with Miss Mary. That's how the trouble started the other night, with him getting notions and tryin' to shine up to her. Driscoll warned him against that, ordered him to stay away from her! And now Driscoll's dead, and you do this—'

'Driscoll's dead because he was a fool!' McKay cut in implacably. 'And he wasn't the only one! The whole crew of you acted like a pack of idiots, Driscoll most of all. He had the notion that because Slash Y runs a lot of cattle, that made him something special—so that anybody with McKay to their name was too good to associate with ordinary folks!' Abe snorted disgustedly. 'Which is the biggest piece of foolishness of all!

'I built Slash Y—startin' from nothing. When I first picked this range for mine, all I had was a couple of scrawny cows and the shirt to my back! Some folks get the notion that havin' a bit of money makes them better than their neighbors, which is plain idiocy. Gordon, I'm askin' you to take on a tough job. You know how tough; you'll be turnin' against your former boss. He'll be fightin' mad and stop at nothing. But you're the only man that's tough enough to stop him. And you've a reason for doing it, after the way he treated you. And that's why I figure maybe you'll take it—because it is a tough job.'

Gordon nodded.

'If you take the job, it'll be up to you,' McKay went on. 'What you say will go. Anybody who don't care to work under those conditions can draw their time. How about it?'

Startled, the truth was borne in upon Gordon. McKay had been looking straight at him, but he hadn't seen the nod. That explained why he'd stuck so close to home these past months, leaving the running of the ranch more and more to Driscoll and Lomax. It wasn't merely that his health was no longer good, his eyesight failing. Buoyed up by an unflinching will, he'd kept going, allowing everyone to assume that he was giving Driscoll a chance to prove himself.

Actually, Abe was blind. Probably the doctor had told him that nothing could be done for him, and he'd accepted the verdict, keeping his own counsel. Complete familiarity with the house, the buildings and paths around Slash Y, coupled with a keen sense of hearing and direction, had enabled him to move around without letting others guess the extent of his affliction.

Gordon did not allow his voice to betray his discovery.

'It sounds like a big order, but if you want me to try, I'll do my best.'

'Fair enough. You're in charge.' Finality was in McKay's pronouncement. 'Lomax, you'll take your orders from him, and so will everyone else. What we have is a fight for existence, for life itself. Under those circumstances, there can't be any division of loyalty.'

'That's right,' Gordon confirmed. 'As a

better man once put it, either we hang together, or we'll hang separately. And in regard to that danger—from now on, when anybody rides, go two and two, not a single man alone, anywhere. And keep alert.' He looked around. Gray was beginning to edge the eastern horizon, and it was too late for anyone to get any sleep that night.

'Let's have some breakfast as soon as possible,' he added. 'We'll have a busy day.'

Somewhat to his surprise, there were no further protests, not even from Lomax. McKay had made his pronouncement, and McKay was still the boss. The disastrous consequences of even a small revolt had sobered them. Gordon turned to where Mary had listened from the background, looking lost and forlorn.

'I'm sorry matters turned out this way,' he told her. 'Mighty sorry.'

Mary nodded uncertainly.

'Thank you,' she replied. 'I keep wondering if what has happened was my fault—if what I did the other evening caused this.' She looked at him directly, and color flowed in a wave back into pale cheeks.

'Papa is pretty blunt sometimes—but he is a judge of men, and I want you to know that I approve his choice of you as foreman. Lomax wasn't big enough for the job, not the way it is now. As for what happened there in the restaurant, I'm afraid I was being foolish, too.

57

I had no idea that you were from Quirt. I supposed of course that you were one of our own crew.'

'I figured you did.'

'If I had realized the situation, I would never have asked you to do something that would get you into trouble the way it did. I just wanted to show that I could be independent, that I had some rights, too. It wasn't that I wanted the beer. I loathe the stuff. But I thought that would show Driscoll.'

Gordon was aware of a long-drawn breath of relief at the explanation. He'd judged her to be a spoiled brat, showing off after her years away at school, with habits which, in his lexicon, real women did not indulge in. Driscoll had felt the same way, and his manner had left her angry and resentful.

'I don't think you have any reason to blame yourself,' Gordon reassured her. 'Quirt had already made up its mind as to its course. O'Dion intends to smash Slash, to take over this whole range. He's been getting ready for a long while, biding his time, knowing that your father was failing. He decided that the time had come, and one of the first necessary steps was to get rid of Driscoll. Other things made no difference.'

'Thank you.' He understood that her appreciation was for the reassurance in regard to what had happened to her brother.

58

'It—will things be bad—the war?'

Gordon nodded soberly. 'Apt to be. O'Dion doesn't start on a venture as big as this unless he thinks he sees his way clear to winning. With Driscoll out of the picture, he'll figure that he can do just about as he pleases.'

He ran fingers wearily through his hair, suddenly conscious of his new responsibility.

'So I'd better start moving. They are apt to strike hard and fast, hoping to catch us all upset and off guard.'

'O'Dion made one bad mistake,' Mary breathed. 'He didn't count on someone like you taking over for us at this juncture! That could turn out to be the worst mistake he ever made!'

CHAPTER SIX

Gordon observed without surprise that the Slash was efficiently run. It was only a short while until the cook issued the call for breakfast. Having missed most of his meals the day before, Brick ate hungrily. The pace of events over the past thirty-six hours made him feel slightly dizzy, despite the dragging interval which he had spent in the bear pit. But he had his thoughts sorted out, a plan in mind, as he scraped back his chair and stood up.

59

'What has happened was all pretty sudden,' he observed. 'And it was just as big a surprise to me as to any of you. I'll say this: O'Dion told everybody on Quirt yesterday that there was going to be war with the Slash. I might have gone along with that, on a fair basis. But when he told us that Quirt was going to steal Slash Y blind, blotching brands as a part of the operation, I asked for my time. He wouldn't give it to me—I suppose he was afraid I'd betray his plans. He didn't aim to let me go.'

The others were listening with interest, but he supplied no details as to how he had walked away despite the ban. They could guess at that.

'Right now, we're all in the same boat. O'Dion intends to fight dirty, and you know what that means. So we'll have to battle for existence. If any of you don't feel like staying, under such conditions, I won't blame you for pulling out now. But for those who stay, we'll go all the way.'

He paused, but no one took advantage of the chance to quit. He'd known that they were a good crew, and loyal; loyal not to him, but to their outfit, to Abe McKay and Mary and the memory of Driscoll. That was as it should be; they'd follow his orders because that was Abe's decision.

'I'd like for you to take one man and go to

town, Lomax,' he went on. 'Make whatever preparations are necessary for the funeral. Driscoll was your friend. Find out from Abe and Mary what they want. For the rest of you, remember what I said about riding in pairs—but don't be trigger-happy. And don't be caught with your guard down.

'Ride the border between Slash and Quirt, and turn back any of our stock which you find anywhere near the line. For the present, we don't want to take chances or lose cattle—especially calves. That's all.'

By rights, he felt that he should confer with Abe, but this was a poor time to bother him. Abe had picked him and told him to do the job.

Looking over the crew, he selected Drake to ride with him. He'd ridden double, behind Drake's saddle, during the night, and found the man likable as well as alert.

Both Quirt and Slash claimed a lot of territory as their respective ranges; between them they occupied the major part of the valley of the Bitter Sage. Bitter Sage Creek rose in the mountains to the west, rolling east and south, picking up tributaries and momentum as it went, until by the time it entered the Slash, it was already a sizable stream.

As a cowboy for Quirt, Gordon had become familiar with the long miles of border, as well as with most of the Slash Y. Across a couple of miles, a deep, almost sheer canyon divided the two outfits, and along that naturally peaceful stretch there had never been any question in regard to boundaries. But on either side of the canyon, for miles in both directions, there was only the creek, winding and twisting, and no firm agreement had ever been reached as to whose range it was.

Abe McKay had been watchful, a formidable opponent, demanding only his rights, but brooking no trespassing. There had never been trouble while Tom Landis was neighbor to Slash, but since the coming of O'Dion, an uneasy truce had prevailed. Now it had been broken.

With Drake jogging beside him, Gordon headed for the section known as the broken arrow. That was a section of low-lying ground, partially wooded, lush with grass, which jutted deep into nominal Quirt territory. The Bitter Sage twisted to the south, took a look at the hills looming as a barrier to its progress, then swung back. In the process it enveloped a thousand acres in the form of an arrow, blunted at the tip. Twice in as many years, O'Dion had protested that the land really belonged to Quirt. Twice he had been rebuffed, and the uneasy *status quo* had been maintained.

Only a couple of days before, Gordon had looked across the wide sprawling creek and observed large herds of Slash Y cattle in the peninsula section, chiefly cows and their calves. He had no doubt that O'Dion knew where every steer, calf or cow belonging to Slash Y was ranging, and he might be ready to take advantage of such an opportunity.

Swarms of tiny gnats clustered in the brush and swarmed around as they rode. The flies of the summer were gone; the tiny insects were a sign of the advancing season. Brush and trees were spending their gold with a lavish recklessness whenever a gust of wind shook them.

With the thick covering of leaves beginning to thin, it was easier to see the stock, or the place where they should have been. Today there was plenty of fresh sign, but nothing more. It took only a few minutes for him to realize that O'Dion had been ahead of them. Not a cow or calf was anywhere on the accustomed range.

There was no particular point in following the twistings and turnings of the creek in a search for sign. All along its length, the cattle were accustomed to drinking, frequently crossing to the other side, just as Quirt stock crossed in turn, mingling the herds. Twice each year at roundup time they were separated, to their manifest bewilderment.

Now, if the cows had been shoved across to Quirt territory, there would be no unusual sign to denote the movement. They might well have been moved the day before.

He explained his fears to Drake, then asked a question.

'Did any of you boys ride this territory yesterday?'

Drake shook his head. 'Maybe Driscoll,' he said. 'All the rest of us were workin' the far end of our range. The only place they could have gone is over there, of course.' He grinned, the smile somewhat strained. 'Do we go over and look for them?'

Gordon shook his head. 'Not today. If we did find them, chances are we'd end up being missing as well. We'll double-check to make sure they're really gone—then, when we cross, we'll go in force.'

Drake nodded approval. 'That's good sense.'

'A day or so won't make much difference now. And we have to give Driscoll a proper burial. I'd prefer to hold off trouble till that's attended to—though I wouldn't count on doing so.'

'Why not?'

'If I know O'Dion, he'll figure the time of the funeral is good to make another move.'

They swung back to the home buildings, riding wide for a look at country where the cows might possibly have strayed. It was unlikely, but Gordon preferred to be sure of his ground before he acted.

The soft haze of Indian summer blanketed the valley in a deceptive calm. While hills and

64

meadows flamed with color, the grass had turned drab. Streams ran softly, though along each one the sign showed an almost frantic flurry of activity among the rodents who called the waterways home. Beavers were putting finishing touches to dams, freshly barked sticks being thrust here and there among the seasoned wood. Willows and cottonwood saplings had been newly felled, towed away and sunk in deep pools to provide winter provender. Muskrats and minks were actuated by the same sense of urgency; their tracks were everywhere in the mud along the shores. In them was the knowledge that such perfect fall weather could not last much longer.

The rest of the crew returned when they did, and there was no good answer to Gordon's questions. The range had been peaceful, but no one had seen the missing cows. Nearly a thousand head had vanished.

The stock must have been rustled while Brick was in the bear pit, cut off from normal sources of information. It helped to explain what had happened to Driscoll. Probably he had sighted the rustlers at work, and had incautiously ventured across to protest. O'Dion was not a man to pass up such an opportunity.

Lomax had made preparations for the funeral, which would be held in town the next day, so that neighbors could attend. It was a last tribute, which would not be neglected and could not be by-passed. The trouble was that O'Dion would probably be ready to take advantage of the diversion, the absence of Slash's crew from their range. Gordon's conviction was so strong that it spoiled his appetite.

He crossed to the big house and found Abe sitting quietly in a chair in the echoing, empty-seeming kitchen. Abe listened to his conclusions, then nodded in agreement.

'Likely you're right,' he conceded. 'O'Dion has waited a long while for a favorable chance, and he thinks it's at hand. Now that he's started, he'll put everything on the board. It is his way.'

Gordon agreed with that assessment. As a gambler, O'Dion had patience and calculation. He'd waited a long while for the right moment. Now he'd go all out.

'You'll understand, then, why I won't be at the funeral tomorrow,' he said.

'I'll understand,' Abe agreed, 'though some may not.'

The hallway was dimly lit by a lamp near its far end. In these shadowy recesses, Gordon encountered Mary. She halted, looking at him questioningly, and he repeated what he had just told her father.

'I thought you should know,' he said.

'That means you'll be off hunting trouble,' Mary returned, 'which you expect will be at hand.'

'I'm afraid it may be. It would be a poor tribute to Driscoll to allow them to bury the rest of us at the same time.'

Her eyes darkened. 'Probably you're right,' she agreed. 'It's all rather terrible. I was so happy to come to the ranch, to be able at last to live here,' she went on. 'I had only visited it twice before in my life, each time for just a few weeks—weeks which never were long enough.'

He listened, with increasing amazement and understanding, as she continued.

'Mother always hated the West, and while she lived, she was determined that I should be kept well away from it, shielded from what she termed its savagery. She lived with Dad for two years out here, and he endured one year back East with her. But neither of them could stand the other's country. Mother had imagination, but only the sort which thought of herself and what she wanted. It was terribly hard on Dad, who'd had big dreams and high hopes when he married her. He was the first to realize that neither of them could change, and he accepted it and didn't complain. And now—now I'm not sure whether I am more his daughter than my mother's, or not.'

The revelation explained many things which had puzzled Gordon. The sudden savage turn of events, so soon after her

67

dreamed-of return, must be hard on her.

'It's rough,' he said, and there was a quality in his voice which made her look up swiftly, then look as quickly away. 'But I don't think you need to worry—certainly not about yourself or how well you'll play your role, no matter how hard the going may become. And I'm sure that having you here is a great comfort to your father. He may not let on, but I know that it means a lot.'

'Thank you,' she murmured. 'He's been disappointed and hurt too many times already. I promise you that he won't be again—not by me. And your confidence helps.'

Gordon was asleep almost before he could crawl into his bunk, but not for long. Even the long ordeal of the bear pit, the sleepless night which had followed, and the tiring day could not keep him asleep long. The problems connected with his new responsibilities brought him awake, and a glance at the moon, shining through the window, told him that he'd slept no more than a couple of hours. Most of the night was still ahead.

He hesitated, hearing the sound of deep breathing or heavy snoring from the other men, mindful that they too had missed their rest the night before. Then, grimly, he reached and shook one man awake.

'Call the others,' he instructed. 'We've a

job to do before the funeral tomorrow—one that O'Dion won't be expecting us to get at so soon—I hope!'

Only one man complained, when he realized the hour, and that work lay ahead. 'Couldn't this job have waited till tomorrow,' he demanded, 'after last night and all?'

'It might have,' Gordon conceded. 'But if I'm guessing right, O'Dion will aim to rid himself of the Slash once and for all. And one burial is plenty.'

Sam Drake was tugging on his boots. 'Unless it's a funeral for Quirt,' he suggested.

'Yeah, unless it's Quirt that's to be buried,' Gordon agreed. 'Let's ride.'

CHAPTER SEVEN

Gordon led out at a brisk trot. He had a good idea as to where the missing cows and calves must have been driven, where they would be held. O'Dion would go ahead according to plans already made; it would hardly occur to him that they could be guessed because Brick Gordon would be with the Slash. He certainly would not expect him to be in charge. O'Dion would logically suppose that, having escaped, Gordon would make the most of his chance to get out of the country, beyond O'Dion's

69

reach.

Well behind the point of the blunted arrow lay a section of Quirt so remote and rough that few even of Quirt's crew knew much about it. Gordon doubted if any outsider was familiar with that stretch. The hills appeared to have been dropped haphazardly, forming a maze. A few miles from the border between Quirt and Slash, there was a hidden meadow of half a hundred acres. It would be perfect for holding the cows and their calves.

The moon was growing old, and like a tired old man it was tardier in its rising, its light fading. They pushed through the broken arrow, hearing the warning slap of a beaver's tail on some remote pond, the rustle of a night bird disturbed by their passage. They were splashing across the Bitter Sage before the moon picked them out.

Shut in by higher hills, it was slow going, but they encountered no sentries. The absence of men on watch seemed a measure of O'Dion's confidence, his assurance that the steps he had already taken gave him control of the situation.

The hills appeared to close solidly, barring further progress. Gordon led the way into a patch of darkness so heavy that the fresh tracks of the missing herd vanished. But a path opened, narrow and twisting, widening suddenly near the meadow. Bathed in the pale glow of the moon, its expanse was dotted with tiny humps made by the sleeping cattle. It was almost bewildering to come upon so large a plot of grassland surrounded by mountains.

The two previous summers that he had worked for Quirt, a herd had always been pushed to this remote fastness, to get the benefit of the grass which otherwise would go uneaten. This year, the meadow had stood virgin, and O'Dion had offered no explanation. Now the reason for saving it was clear.

The faint smell of burnt wood, a lingering odor of scorched hair and hide assailed the nostrils. A blackened spot, with fragments of charred wood remaining, gave mute testimony that branding had taken place there within the last day or so.

'Let's have a look at them,' Gordon said.

Riding among the stock, rousing them to stand and blink in sleepy astonishment at the sight of horsemen abroad at that hour, it did not take long to confirm his guess, or to see how O'Dion had already carried out his threat. The cows were all branded Slash Y. Once awakened, both they and their offspring seemed jittery and hostile. It was easy to guess that they had been slow to settle down for the night.

A considerable crew, probably composed of most of the men of Quirt, had been busy among them during the day. Most of the

71

calves had been branded. Unlike their mothers, the blisteringly fresh scars on their skins showed the sign of the Quirt.

Though some of the Slash had expected something of the sort, the magnitude of the steal caused them to exclaim incredulously. The awakened calves huddled close to their mothers, but nothing could hide the new burns.

'Does that so and so think he can get away with this?' Drake demanded in astonishment. 'Why, if the rest of the people—the men from the small outfits, and the town, saw what we're seein' now—'

'That's what we want them to see,' Gordon observed grimly. 'Quirt didn't count on anyone stumbling on them back in here. And after a few days, of course, the calves would be put off by themselves and the cows allowed to drift back to their own range. And then anybody could see the brands, but who could prove anything?'

The magnitude of the theft was breath-taking. This was most of the calf crop of Slash, whose loss could come close to ruining their owners. As O'Dion had intimated the other morning, he wasn't contenting himself with piecemeal rustling, which would merely invite trouble and bring no definite results. He was moving to destroy the Slash, deliberately taking a course which would cause retaliation and so furnish an excuse for further, totally cripping blows. The belief that he had gotten away with the first two moves—disposing of Driscoll McKay and now the calves—would embolden him.

'Round them up and get them moving,' Gordon instructed. 'We'll take them home.'

The crew eyed him with new respect as they set to work. Some had resented being roused for night work so soon after hitting the hay, and following a sleepless night. Here was proof that he'd known what he was about. If they could get the herd back on Slash Y range, then bring in outsiders to view the evidence of misbranded calves still running with Slash mothers—O'Dion would be in an untenable position.

It would not be easy, for the cattle were as weary as the men, and disinclined to keep moving when they should be resting. The excitement and confusion of branding, of moving to a strange pasture, had kept them at an exhausting pitch. Now they looked upon every man with suspicious hostility.

Still they moved, and as the cows sensed that they were heading back for the home range, some of their reluctance vanished. It was off here, on alien ground, that trouble had come upon them. There was reassurance in the familiar.

Gordon had not made the same mistake as O'Dion by failing to post lookouts. It was unlikely that anyone would be around to see or hear, for the buildings on Quirt were a long way off, but he'd allowed himself to be caught off guard a couple of times, and he couldn't afford a third case of laxity. He'd posted a couple of watchers on high ground, and now one of them came spurring.

'Quirt's awake and on the move,' he reported breathlessly. 'The first thing I noticed was a light, then a lot of them, off at their place. Next thing I made out the crew, saddlin' up. The moon hits there, so I could see all right. It looked to me like the whole crew was on the move—and I reckon they'll be headin' to cut us off!'

The luck they'd had already had seemed too good to last. Apparently O'Dion must have had someone posted and on watch, after all. Instead of making the mistake of challenging them when they had appeared, the sentry had high-tailed it back with word of what was going on; that would give Quirt plenty of time to intercept them short of the line.

Gordon's scalp crawled. This was the sort of showdown he'd hoped to avoid, at least at this stage of the game. Now it appeared to be inevitable. Unless they deserted the herd and fled ignominiously, a pitched battle could result. Quirt, under such circumstances, could do nothing else.

In such a clash, many men on both sides

would die. Since crews were fairly well matched in both size and ability, the battle might well end in a virtual draw. Both sides would be losers, writing one more bloody chapter in range warfare, with the final result still in doubt.

'You're sure they're out to stop us?' he demanded, and realized that the question sounded inane. What else could bring Quirt from their beds at that hour, to ride in force?

'They were just startin' away from the buildings when I headed here to warn you,' the sentry explained. 'I don't know what else they'd have in mind.'

It was a slender enough chance, yet the possibility that they might have some other purpose was worth exploring. O'Dion had been confident and complacent, and there had been no other sign of a sentry being posted to watch the cows. Gordon's notion became a hunch.

'Come along with me,' he instructed the sentry. 'The rest of you, keep the herd moving.'

He rode fast, pushing his horse up the steepening incline which lay between them and the buildings, his hunch deepening almost to a conviction. Their purpose now might be something else; in fact, it almost had to be. Had someone been posted to keep an eye on the cattle, he could hardly have gotten back to the buildings and roused the sleepers so quickly. The only way in which they could have been warned at such speed would have been by firing a gun as a signal, and that had not been done.

Brush hindered and branches whipped at them as Gordon kept the horses at a headlong pace. Then they topped the rise, to the point where the lookout had been. The buildings at Quirt once more stood dark and remote, the lights all gone out. The band of riders, in close formation, were a mile away, moving steadily.

Studying them, Gordon's eyes lightened. His companion swore in bewilderment.

'Now what in tarnation are they up to?' he demanded. 'That's a funny course they're takin'—if they're aimin' to cut us off.'

'I doubt if they have any such idea in mind,' Gordon returned. 'Likely they don't suspect that we're here at all.'

'Then what are they up to?'

The answer would have been highly useful, but Gordon could only speculate as to what O'Dion might have in mind, though he had a good hunch. The funeral was to be held in town, toward noon. Judging from the course which the crew of Quirt were now taking, they clearly were not heading for Long Rain.

'My guess is that they plan to finish Slash off while our back is turned,' he explained. 'If they keep on that way, they can be posted, say within a mile of our buildings, and be ready to move in as soon as our crew rides for town. That would give them a choice—either to burn us out, or to take over and stand us off when we get back. Either way, on top of all the rest, it would just about finish us.'

Quinsell removed his hat to scratch his head, as though requiring some extra deep thinking.

'By golly, I'd say you've hit it,' he conceded. 'Only we won't be there to ride out, the way they expect.' He replaced the hat, scowling as he pursued this line of thought. 'But they'll see Abe and Miss Mary start off for town, as well as Jack and the cook—so they'll know we ain't there. Which'll suit them just as well, though it might give them some new ideas.'

Quinsell's conclusion matched his own line of reasoning, and Gordon didn't like it. Quirt must be stopped short of their objective. How that could be managed, without having Quirt upon their own necks at the wrong time, was not so easy to determine.

A gunshot now would attract Quirt's attention, and it would bring not only an investigation but also an attack. Since a battle to a finish would be weighted in Quirt's favor, it had to be avoided, except as a last resort.

It would be possible to split his own crew, sending the majority of them back to the buildings. Several things were wrong with that idea, the main trouble being that it was already too late. Riding straight and fast, they might beat the invaders, but they would be seen, and again attack would follow. Should they circle to avoid being seen, they would arrive too late.

'That's a blasted dirty way to fight, if you ask me—' Quinsell said savagely—'to jump an outfit when they're buryin' a man!'

'What they're interested in is buryin' *us*,' Gordon reminded him. 'O'Dion didn't get where he is by playing nice.'

Quinsell shrugged, eying him expectantly. He had considered the possibilities which were open to them, and had reached the same doubtful conclusions. The single reassuring factor was that Gordon was boss here, and making a decision was his responsibility. If he could come up with a workable plan, he'd be a genius.

Gordon's glance strayed back to the huddle of buildings, which now stood deserted and unguarded. O'Dion's thinking was perfectly logical. Because Driscoll McKay was the son of old Abe, it was natural that the whole crew should do him one final honor by attending hs funeral. Thus their whereabouts could be accurately judged at any hour of the day. Most of Slash Y's neighbors would also attend. Thus it seemed perfectly safe to leave Quirt unguarded.

But there was a flaw in such reasoning, and

if he could find a way to take advantage of it—

Gordon shook his head at the obvious. It would be easy to ride over there now and set fire to the buildings. The rising smoke would soon be seen, as daylight came, and duly interpreted by the riders of Quirt, before they were ready to make their own attack. Presumably, faced with such a situation, most of them would head back in a hurry in an effort to save what they could.

They would be too late, and such a loss would be a blow to Quirt, weakening but still not crippling them. Moreover, that was the sort of fighting which Gordon hated. He'd asked for his time when O'Dion had announced his intention of going outside the law; practicing arson on such a scale would be equally criminal.

Worse, he doubted if burning the buildings would achieve its purpose. By the time the Quirt riders sighted the smoke, O'Dion might decide, from its magnitude, that his own buildings were already past saving. He might send some men back; but being a realist, he'd probably keep on with most of them, seizing the Slash Y and holding the buildings for living quarters. Such a plan would backfire.

Yet there might be a third course. It was a gambler's choice, but this clearly was a time for risks. Gordon outlined his plan, and Quinsell nodded.

'Watch for my signal; then help attract their attention,' Gordon emphasized. 'I'll do the rest.' Swinging his horse, he headed for the vacant buildings on Quirt.

CHAPTER EIGHT

The hour could be counted either late, or early, as Gordon approached Quirt. The moon, having hovered uncertainly in the Indian summer sky, had become entangled among the spire-like mountains to the west. There was a sharp chill to the air, and a coating of frost was visible on both leaves and bare ground. The long spell of fine weather still held, but he'd detected a cloudy circle beyond the moon, one more indication that winter might be expected at any time.

The waning of the moon might in itself be the signal for storms. A full moon frequently had the effect of thinning clouds, holding back rain or snow. But when it thinned in turn, they took their revenge. The pattern seemed discouragingly similar to the contest in the valley of the Bitter Sage.

It still lacked an hour to dawn, and any men who might have been left behind would be sleeping more soundly than ever, after being disturbed by the departure of the others. The cook would probably be counting on the rare luxury of sleeping late, knowing that for once he wouldn't have to prepare breakfast.

Familiar as he was with everything about Quirt, Gordon was able to move without waste of time. He was tempted to go to the bunk house after some of his own things, but there was no time. The plan would be touch and go at best, timed desperately close.

The big house towered, shadowy and huge, above the other buildings, a vast pile of stone erected to the vanity of O'Dion. Gordon knew that it was more a monument to pride than a home in which to live; similar to the edifices which the rulers of ancient lands had caused to be built by enslaved multitudes. Fire might gut the house, but it wouldn't really burn.

Yet there was a way to destroy it, and it would hit O'Dion hard, right in his pride.

At the back of the house, almost lost in its shadow, stood another stone building. This was a storehouse, built originally as a root-house, also a part of O'Dion's dream. There had been a root-house on the farm when he was a boy, so he'd had to have one here. Not until it had been built had it occurred to him that it would be useless for that purpose, since no vegetables were grown on Quirt, nor were any cows milked; therefore there was no need to keep cream and butter in a cool place.

As a storehouse it was solid, the walls and

roof a couple of feet in thickness. There was no window, and only one door, of heavy planks. O'Dion had built well, if foolishly.

The door was held shut by a stick thrust through a heavy iron hasp. Gordon removed the stick and pushed the door open. Inside, everything was as he remembered it, untouched since his last visit to the building, months before. At that time, since he possessed a skill unknown to most cowboys, he'd done some blasting for O'Dion, blowing a dam and constructing a reservoir. The waters which until then had run to waste now formed a considerable lake. It was O'Dion's plan to irrigate a thousand normally dry acres.

Several hundred-pound cans of black blasting powder and a box, still crammed with sticks of dynamite, had been left over from these operations, stored back in this strong room. There was also a supply of caps and fuse.

Gordon worked swiftly, measuring a long length of fuse, able to judge from past experience. The heavy padlock, which had not been in the hasp, was on a table. The key, in a ring along with several others, hung from a peg, driven into a crack between the stones of the wall.

Disregarding the key, Gordon took the lock, then lit the fuse. Outside, he fitted the lock in the hasp and snapped it shut. Now he had set in motion a chain of events which had to be timed right, or he'd have unloosed a demon which would really turn the sage bitter.

Remembering the agreed-upon signal, he lifted his revolver and sent two quick shots toward the fading stars.

Somewhere in the hills the echo came back, with a quavery, uncertain quality. Then, like a new and grimmer echo, two more shots disturbed the serenity of the night, from a greater distance. That would be Quinsell.

Gordon pushed his cayuse to its limit.

Even at that, he was barely in time, with nothing to spare, when he sighted the herd. They had halted when the guns sounded. Until then, his crew had kept them on the move, covering half the distance between the hidden meadow and the jut of Bitter Sage Creek which marked the uneasy boundary with Slash Y.

Here, the hills and timber which clothed that section of range had thinned, opening into a long valley. Night still clung relentlessly, the high stars giving a scant but sufficient light.

Hearing the shots, O'Dion's crew had reacted as he'd anticipated, swinging to investigate. Guns sounding in the dark of night were unusual, and with relations so troubled, they might be significant.

It hadn't taken them long to sight Quinsell;

then, as he fled in apparent panic at being discovered, they had chased him, soon coming in sight of the herd. At that juncture it was natural to put two and two together. If they failed to add correctly, they could still be excused for believing the obvious, the evidence of their own eyes.

They were riding hard, startled, to stop the cows and their calves from returning to Slash Y. The tables had been partially turned, a surprise handed O'Dion, but he was ready to meet the challenge, even though it meant altering his own plan. It could be disastrous to allow such evidence on the hoof to get back for others to see. Now, if Slash wanted a showdown, this time and place suited him well enough.

Somewhat startled by the sudden appearance of the crew of Quirt, Lomax was gathering his own men for the expected clash. In Gordon's absence, he was in charge and ready to make a fight of it.

One of the men sighted the lone rider, and being more relieved than discreet, exclaimed loudly:

'Here comes Gordon!'

Not only did they hear, but in the stillness of the night, Quirt was close enough to hear, too. Momentarily, as though sensing an approaching climax, even the cows and their misused offspring had fallen silent; not a single forlorn bawl disturbed the night. To the east, a smudge of light was fumbling uncertainly at the curtain of blackness, trying to tear a hole in it.

Quirt was fairly close by now. Lomax had instructed his men to hold their fire, hoping to parley instead of shoot, though without much hope that talk would do any good. At this stage, neither side could afford to back down or even compromise, and the Slash had no intention of doing so. But neither outfit wanted to bear the onus of starting a shooting war, without at least an attempt at discussion. Blood would spill soon enough.

Both groups pulled up, not far apart, looking to Gordon as he came between them. He stopped, and the sobbing breath of his cayuse was the only sound for a moment. O'Dion leaned forward, peering in the uncertain light, and exclaimed in disbelief.

'Gordon! Now what the devil are you doing here?'

'That is a good question, which might work both ways,' Gordon observed innocently. 'But to save time, which is crowding us, and especially you, I'll tell you. I'm rodding Slash Y.'

He saw the incredulity on his former employer's face give way to amusement, followed a moment later by a shout of laughter.

'What's that you're tellin' me, that you're roddin' the Slash? You! Tryin' to fill the

85

boots of Abe McKay, to take the place of Driscoll, thinkin' now you'll have a clear field with the girl and win Slash Y for yourself! So that is it! Now, by all that's rich—'

'Shut up and listen.' The incisiveness of Gordon's voice cut through the laughter, and despite himself, O'Dion listened. Gordon went on quickly.

'There's not a minute to lose, O'Dion, if you want to save your buildings. And you know that I know what I'm talking about in regard to explosives. When I saw what you were up to, I headed there and lit a fuse in the storehouse. There's more than enough dynamite and powder in that pile to blow your fine big house to sand, and the fire would take all the rest of the buildings.'

Slowly, the dawn light was picking out objects, whitening the frost underfoot. In the brightness, O'Dion's face lost its ruddiness.

'Why, you—you—' he choked.

'Listen,' Gordon insisted. 'You'll have time to save your place, providing you get back there, fast, you and your whole crew. I used a long fuse, and timed it close, but I allowed enough. The door's padlocked—and the key is still inside, on its nail, out of reach!'

He gave O'Dion a moment in which to digest that, to come to a full understanding. O'Dion himself had selected that padlock, making sure that it was huge and solid. Even a volley of shots from a gun would have little effect on it.

Originally there had been two keys. But one of those had been lost. Now, with the other locked inside the building—

'How the devil can I get to it, if you've left it inside?' O'Dion snarled.

'If you want to save your place, you'll have to work for it.' Gordon shrugged. 'Otherwise it would be too easy, and you might try to do too many other things also. Remember that big log lying near the barn? Use it as a battering ram. Carried by your whole crew, it will smash even that door in time for you to put out the fuse. But you'll have to ride fast, every man of you!'

O'Dion's face twisted thoughtfully as he understood. How it could have happened he was far from comprehending, just as it was incomprehensible that this man, whom he'd had thrown into the bear pit, could have escaped, and now be directing the opposition, with Slash Y following his leadership.

Yankus had reported the escape of Gordon, but O'Dion had been sure that Gordon, scared but thankful to be alive, would have left the country. He had been equally certain that Slash Y, with Driscoll McKay about to be buried, would be disorganized, virtually leaderless, and easy to take over. The shock of the discovery to the contrary was hard to take.

The other was equally bitter. His plan to

seize control of the buildings on the Slash while the crew was absent was suddenly spoiled; worse, his own headquarters, including the house which he prized so much, was in danger of destruction. Knowing Gordon, he did not for a moment doubt that he was telling the truth.

Gordon's manner of hitting back, seizing control of the initiative, was equally unpleasant. There was no time left for argument or counter-action. Nor was the threat lost upon him or his pale-faced crew. If they were even a second tardy, the dynamite might blow up in their faces, enveloping them in the destruction.

Still worse, the showdown which he had been savoring would have to be postponed. The calves, tagging at their mothers' heels, with those damaging, damning brands on their flanks, would have to be be permitted to cross back to Slash Y range, where an outraged public could see and judge. Such exposure might well spell the end to an inglorious adventure.

'You're a fine one!' O'Dion choked. 'To hit at a man in such fashion—sneaking behind his back—'

'Now that's interesting, coming from you, O'Dion,' Gordon taunted. 'I wonder where you were riding just now, and what you might have had in mind!' O'Dion gulped, and he went on.

'The thing which amazes and shames me is that I worked for you so long! But I'm striving to make restitution, and I'm also giving you a chance to do the same, to save your house. I could just as easily have used a short fuse.'

The truth of that was so manifest that O'Dion swallowed his pride and some of his rage, clapping spurs to his horse and leading his crew in a desperate race. The thunder of the blast, at such a juncture, would have accomplished what smoke alone could not have done, and sent him and his men scurrying back too late. In his present mood, he felt no gratitude for the chance which was offered.

As the dust settled behind the departing Quirt, Gordon lifted an arm, and the drive went on, into the face of the rising sun.

CHAPTER NINE

By now, sensing the nearness of home, the cows stepped out briskly, anxious to be gone from this range which had been so full of trouble. Wearily, Gordon tried to plan his next move, but his mind, like his body, was too tired to respond well. It had been a long night, following another without sleep, but the results were worth it. The trouble was that endurance had a limit, and all of them were close to the breaking point.

Had he failed to follow his hunch, today would have marked the end for Slash Y, as well as for many of those who rode for it. O'Dion had come close to pulling it off.

He strained his ears, and it was not until they had crossed the creek onto Slash Y range that he could ease the breath in his lungs, certain that his gamble had not ended in a desperate holocaust. He'd tried to time everything right, but with so many factors involved, there had been room for error, human or otherwise. If O'Dion had arrived too late to save his house, but only in time to witness its destruction—

Or worse, if they had gotten there to be caught by the blast—

That, of course, would settle everything, assuring victory to Slash Y. Nor did he have any doubts that the public, the men on the other ranches and in town, would exonerate them once they heard the story and viewed the misbranded calves. The trouble would be that he'd never be able to free himself of the horror, the memory of men blasted and maimed because of what he'd done.

It was better this way, though the real war was just beginning. O'Dion was not a man to draw back in gratitude, because Brick had given him a chance to save his house. Instead, he'd dwell on the defeat he'd suffered, the humiliation of being forced to jump at Gordon's command, the risk they'd run while the flame along the fuse crept desperately close to the explosives. Had there been any doubt before, the night's events had removed it. It would be war now, war to a finish. Nothing else would salve the flayed pride of O'Dion.

It was day now, the day of the funeral, one scheduled to be set apart for mourning, for paying the last and proper respects to a man untimely and feloniously dead. Most of the neighbors could be counted on to take time off to attend, not so much out of liking or respect for the dead man himself as for his father. Abe McKay had been raised in a hard school, and he was blunt-spoken, short with sympathy for the foolish or the inept. He'd expressed the common sentiment when declaring that his son had acted like a fool.

But deep down, everyone knew that Abe McKay was a man who had suffered disillusion and a shattering of dreams when his wife had refused to live in a country which she termed barbaric, taking his tiny daughter and returning to the East to her folks. What attempts, beyond his own year in the East, Abe might have made to set matters right, no one knew or ever would. He was not one to talk about himself or his troubles. He had returned to the only life he knew, to the ranch he'd taken and was determined to hold; to the only place where he fitted. There, alone, he had raised his son the best way he knew.

Somewhere along the way he felt that he'd botched the job; or perhaps the fault had lain partly with Driscoll. In him had been the same unseemly pride, the same flaw of character that had manifested itself in his mother, a self-centeredness which took no account of others, either their wishes or their rights. Driscoll had been a disappointment, and when his father had needed him most, the son had derided him, making a grab for power.

Now it had brought him to his grave, and almost everyone would attend the funeral, the gesture one of sympathy and understanding for the living; for Abe, and for Mary, who showed promise of being sturdy and unspoiled, despite her mother's training.

It would be natural for a raging O'Dion to use the day for his own purposes. So to take chances would be folly.

Brick asked Lomax to go with Abe and Mary to the funeral, 'to make sure that nothing happens to them.'

Lomax's astonishment showed in his face.

'You mean—you're leavin' it up to me to look out for them? I'd sort of supposed—'

'It's important, and I'll be busy with other things. I figure that Slash comes first, with both of us.'

Lomax swallowed. He was grateful for this

show of confidence, and his words came impulsively.

'Sure,' he agreed. 'That's right enough. And I'm glad that you're handlin' matters now, instead of me. That was a stroke of genius, the way you managed tonight.'

A haze was spreading over the sky, beginning to blot away the early sun. Gordon scanned the horizon apprehensively, testing the feel of the air. Normally, a heavy frost was followed by a fine day, but after a prolonged spell of good weather, anything might be expected. The feverish activity of the wild seemed to be accounted for. A change was on the way, and when it struck, winter was apt to hit with full fury.

Breakfast over, he outlined the situation to the others.

'We can't risk leaving this place unguarded, especially when it would seem safe to do so. A third of the crew can represent the rest of us at the funeral. The rest of us will stay, taking turns at keeping watch and getting some sleep.'

Lomax drove a two-seated buggy as the cortege set out for town. Abe McKay and Mary were on the rear seat, wrapped in a heavy buffalo robe. Even with gloves, fingers stiffened, and breath began to blow frostily from the nostrils of horses and men alike. The brief sun had vanished.

Despite the imminence of a storm, it

seemed as though everyone for a wide radius had turned out for the funeral. As the casket was lowered into the ground, Lomax was surprised to see O'Dion at the edge of the crowd, head bared like the others, his face solemn. He was the only one from Quirt to be seen.

Standing beyond O'Dion was the sheriff, a blocky figure in a heavy bearskin coat. Lomax scowled, made his decision. As soon as the service ended, he moved to intercept Harder, steering him toward his employer.

'Abe wants a word with you, Harder,' he explained.

Harder moved restively, as though guessing what that word might be. Then he followed, stumping along impatiently.

'I got a lot to do,' he protested. 'I took time off to come out here, but I'm a busy man.'

'Likely,' Lomax agreed laconically. 'But Abe's got something for you in the line of business.'

'Well?' Harder halted, spitting out the word truculently. 'What is it, McKay?'

McKay's Scotch ancestry was evident in the dryness of his reply.

'It's a comfort, now, to have a man in your place who is as chary of wasting time as money. If you'll come to the ranch, we've something to show you. Evidence, fresh burned on many a calf's tender skin; brand blotching.'

94

'What's this you're saying?' Harder sounded incredulous. 'Has your brand been overlaid with another, or altered with a running iron?'

'Nothing like that. These are new brands on calves which had no burn before; calves still running with their mothers, who wear the Slash. So if you will come and see for yourself—'

The sheriff shied like a cayuse catching a whiff of grizzly.

'To make such a trip right now is out of the question,' he said flatly. 'I'm in the middle of another job. If you have such evidence as you say, it will keep.'

'So will a rotten egg,' Lomax cut in angrily. 'Only it gets worse the longer it stays around.'

Harder favored him with a stare of manifest dislike.

'I run my job my way,' he grunted, and stalked off.

'He'd been confabbin' with O'Dion just before I talked to him,' Lomax explained to Gordon. By now, the clouds had pulled down tightly all around the horizon, the wind was whetting its edge across the broad wastes to the north, and a few flakes of snow were beginning to push like wary outriders of an advancing army. 'Likely enough that was O'Dion's only reason for showin' up there.'

Gordon nodded. O'Dion had made certain hat he would have no trouble from the law before making his move. If there was evidence, Harder would find some pretext not to take a look, at least until it was too late to matter.

Gordon had slept for a couple of hours, and felt ready for whatever might come. He could go a long way without much rest. The rest of the crew were not so well off. Two sleepless nights in succession, along with the emotional strain, were taking a toll. Many of them were all but walking in their sleep.

That posed a dilemma. That O'Dion was also caught upon its horns was scant consolation, for he could be counted on to resort to desperate measures to get off. So many new-branded calves, running with cows of another brand, posed a serious threat. Even though the law refused to have a look, others would ride to view them as soon as the storm had blown itself out.

At the moment that was the big problem. Already the snow was choking the air, reducing visibility to a few dozen feet. It would be a bad night to be out.

Gordon would have liked to move both cows and calves to the home corrals, where they could be held and watched, during the day. But doing so had been out of the question. There were far too many to be held in the corrals, and they were too tired to drive any farther. They, too, would have to wait out the storm.

He could post guards, but in a black night, sentries would be useless and helpless. The worst part was that there was no one fit to send.

He crossed to the house and found Mary washing the supper dishes for her father and herself. She turned, wiping her hands on her apron. Outside, it was already dark. The beat of the storm was steady against the windows, the wind howling, moaning. She managed a tired smile.

'Jim told us how you checkmated O'Dion,' she said. 'He was proud of you—and so am I!'

'That was a lucky break, that dynamite being in the right place and needing only a match to the fuse,' Gordon returned. 'I had only to take advantage of it.'

'Perhaps, but not everyone would have thought of such a thing, or known how to make use of the chance,' she returned. 'It won over all those who had been resentful or doubtful, even Lomax.'

'It was luck,' Gordon repeated. 'It's tomorrow that I'm worried about.'

'Tomorrow?' She gestured to the window, where the beat of flinty pellets made a steady rattle. 'But you'll be ready to move if they do, after a good night's sleep. And you've certainly earned it.'

'What I mean is, O'Dion may have something waiting for us by the time morning comes. He's desperate, and he's that sort of a man.'

'But what can he do? Surely it's too black and bad a night for anyone to be abroad in—'

'It would seem so,' Gordon acknowledged. 'On the other hand, a night like this would be a perfect cover. He knows that our men are played out, that they must sleep tonight.'

'But his men must be tired, too.'

'They could have slept today,' he pointed out. 'Still, I'll not borrow trouble—that would be foolish, when there's plenty already. I just wanted to make sure that you and your father were all right.'

'I'm all right,' Mary assured him. 'Papa's asleep already—this had been hard on him, though he doesn't let on. He feels that with you looking after things, matters will come out all right. I don't know how we'd manage without you.'

'There's nothing for me to brag about—yet,' he protested, suddenly diffident. 'I'm sorry that this has been so hard on you.'

She turned, facing him directly, and he saw that in her face which stilled his words. There was something of the calmness of her father's expression.

'What happened to Driscoll was dreadful, of course,' she told him. 'I'm sorry, as we all are. But for the rest, we have to face up to life, and I learned long ago that it's no use to try to run from it. That was Mother's mistake, and by that attitude, she almost ruined a lot of lives, including her own. It's hard, many times, but we can do what has to be done. Besides, I feel just as Papa does. With you in charge, things will come out all right.'

He scarcely felt the storm as he moved across to the bunk house, her words still sounding in his ears, her promise a soft gleam in her eyes. She had made a declaration of faith, faith in him rather than in the situation. Given such an incentive, a man could hardly fail.

CHAPTER TEN

Daylight brought no indication of any let-up in the storm. During the night, it had become a full-fledged blizzard, despite the earliness of the season. Snow lay everywhere, and more was coming, buffeted and shifted by the wind. Drifts were already growing deep. Other sections, swept free of cover, seemed to shiver in the cold. The ground had turned frozen and unyielding.

Wild weather presented problems for cattlemen. The older stock would be all right for a while, but the cows with calves still at heel would need to be moved in closer, fed with hay from the stacks put up during the summer. Gordon was in the saddle as soon as it was light enough to see, with half the crew beside him.

Tired as he had been, he hadn't slept well; he'd dreamed and turned, haunted by a sense of impending disaster. He pushed his horse hard, anxious to learn the worst, hoping that his hunch was wrong. Reason was on his side, but some people had a way of doing the unreasonable.

Again, as on an earlier occasion, the vacancy of the broken arrow hit them as they crossed it. They clung to a faint hope, since the cows might be huddled in little bunches in the coulees and brush, waiting out the storm. Few creatures, even such hardy wanderers as coyotes, ventured abroad on such a day.

As though conjured up by the thought, they heard the sound of a coyote, the howl lifting wraith-like. In response, a cow bawled, then another. That should have been reassuring, for the cows were there. Instead, the sound was keyed to a troubled pitch, lost and mournful, different from the complaining note of the previous day.

Something moved, and Brick swung his horse that way. It was a coyote, slinking guiltily, after gnawing at something in the snow. Gordon bent to examine it, and Lomax came to join him.

'What the devil?' Lomax asked, staring in disbelief. He stirred the partly frozen mass with the toe of a boot, turning a blank face to Gordon. 'It's not a cow—or a calf. But it looks like one had been gutted here.'

'That's about what it is,' Gordon agreed tightly, and swung back to the saddle, suspicion mounting to a dreadful certainty. The day was rawly cold, almost numbing after the mild weather which had prevailed until the previous evening. It would require at least a couple of days for men and animals to grow accustomed to the change.

Not far away, they found another similar mass of partly frozen remains. Then they came upon several cows, and by now the chorus of complaint sounded louder, rising from many throats. The cows, plastered with snow which cracked but clung when they moved, regarded them with hostility. Their udders hung full. Nowhere was there a sign of a calf.

Additional searching yielded further confirmation. It verged on the incredible, yet it was past doubting. There were no calves with brands which failed to match those of their mothers. But there were far too many piles of entrails, despite the feasting coyotes. The calves had been butchered, then the hides and meat hauled away.

This could spell catastrophe for Slash Y. Gordon stared glumly. He'd feared some sort of a counter-move by O'Dion, but nothing of this sort had occurred to him. He would have said that under the circumstances it was out of the question; there had been so many calves, so black a night with driving storm.

But O'Dion had matched his own impossible feat of the day before, simply by refusing to concede that it couldn't be done, then by making an all-out effort. He'd had two things going for him: the first being the certainty that Slash Y would have to get some sleep; the other the chance for his own men to sleep the day before and ready themselves for a rough, hard night.

His crew had responded to the challenge. Whatever else they might be, Quirt's crew were loyal to their boss, especially when faced with a danger which, unless remedied, could threaten their necks.

In one respect, the storm had been their ally. On open range, cattle would drift with a storm, but here, where there was shelter, cows and calves had huddled, almost unmoving, reluctant even to stir. Also, the snow, added to the night, would have afforded a cover in which the gleam of lanterns would have been invisible except close at hand.

Looking closer, it was possible to find additional sign, where the snow had been whipped aside, or along the creek, where in the brush it was barely ruffled by the wind. Additional snowfall had partly covered the tracks of wheels, but not entirely. Wagons, a lot of them, had been brought in, loaded with the veal meat and stripped, telltale hides, then moved out again, taking the evidence with them.

Brutally efficient, the crew of Quirt, implemented by extra hands whom O'Dion had hired in anticipation of some emergency action, had moved among the herd, some of them carrying lanterns. The stir and bustle throughout much of the night had not been enough to stampede the cows. Men on horseback could check such attempts, turning back or holding any who tried to get away. Between darkness and daylight, they had been able to do a remarkably thorough job.

The calves, of course, had been slain in the quickest, simplest and quietest manner. They had been knocked on the head with an axe, then bleeded and gutted, after which the hides were quickly stripped off, meat and hides slung onto the waiting wagons.

Gordon could envision what a tremendous operation it had been. A big crew had worked hard, under adverse conditions. But the evidence showed that it had been done.

So far, they had failed to discover a single remaining calf with the telltale Quirt brand. The evidence of the sides was gone, along with the meat. The cold, with the temperature steadily dropping, had made the operation feasible. The frozen meat would keep until it could be taken to a market, thus making the night's work a financial success—something which always bulked large in O'Dion's planning. At the same time, though he had failed to acquire the calves to fatten the big herd on Quirt, they had been taken away from Slash, which had been his main objective.

To try and drive them back onto Quirt range would have been a hopeless task, besides, it would have been impossible to hide them from a search. Stragglers would have fallen out all along the line and not have been missed in the darkness.

This way, the evidence was gone. What remained—cows mourning for their calves, the refuse from butchered animals—was being buried by the storm, as well as eaten by wolves, coyotes, magpies and other scavengers. In any case, it was not proof which could be used against any one. No brands or marks of identification had been left behind.

The real reason for O'Dion's attendance at the funeral was explained. Using it as a cover, he'd been able to pass the word, marshaling his extra men, wagons, teams and whatever was required for the night's operation.

As the manner and extent of the catastrophe were understood, the other Slash riders were swearing, exclaiming in anger and incredulity.

'But they can't get away with it!' Lomax

exclaimed. 'We'll be able to come up with the wagons—and the evidence. They can't move fast enough to outrun us.'

The same thought was in Gordon's mind. Laden wagons could be followed and overtaken. It would mean trouble when they caught up, the showdown which had been averted the day before. But it was no longer a matter of choice.

The others were all for instant pursuit, but Gordon checked the rush for horses. If and when they caught up, they'd be faced with a strong, hostile force; inevitably, they'd need every man that it was possible to muster for such a contest.

On the other hand, O'Dion had schemed and planned for a long while, and last night, as the evidence indicated, he must have recruited a lot of additional men to his standard. Not only would they outnumber the Slash in an encounter, but he undoubtedly would have a force in reserve, ready to hit at the buildings on Slash if they were left unguarded. A second crippling blow, such as burning them out, with winter suddenly blasting the country, would just about finish them.

Gordon pointed this out. Lomax scowled, but agreed reluctantly.

'We'll have to leave those who are there to stay on guard,' Gordon said. 'As for the rest of us—when we catch up, we'll have to fight that much harder.'

'Well, what of it?' Sam Drake growled. 'Let's get at it!' The others nodded assent.

They rode, a grim and silent group, fully aware what might await them. Quirt's crew, guarding the wagons, would be riding those same wagons, sheltered under heavy buffalo robes, warm and ready for action. That would give them a tremendous advantage over men half-numb from long hours in the saddle, whose hands and feet had scarcely any feeling.

Yet time was of the essence. Unless they overtook them, and with the evidence, it would be too late.

The storm showed no let-up as the day wore on. It would probably last at least through the night, and the drivers of the wagons, taking advantage of its cover, would do their best to lose the pursuit. They were probably experiencing some uneasy moments at the thought of vengeance riding hard in their wake.

Despite wind and blowing snow, the tracks of several wagons could not be fully covered. The trail became easier to follow, though except for that trace of sign, and themselves, the road seemed deserted. They had come out upon a road, leaving Quirt behind, swinging off toward the south. A part of O'Dion's intention was becoming clear.

Beyond, deep in the mountains, a large

construction camp was located, consisting of a combined logging and mining operation. It had been there, on a small scale, for more than a year. During the summer, the operators had made two important moves. One had consisted in bringing in and setting up a sawmill, to cut logs into rough lumber. Getting finished lumber out was far easier than transporting logs to a mill, where water was not available to run them.

The mining operation had also prospered, with the rich vein they had hoped for finally being located. Now the camp had mushroomed, and would afford a ready and eager market for even several wagonloads of newly butchered meat. More to the point, they could be counted on to buy, and no questions asked.

O'Dion must have planned for most possible eventualities. With Slash Y forced to improvise against him, that left the odds increasingly on the side of Quirt.

It was midday when they finally sighted the wagons, a long line of them, crawling through the gloom of the storm, each wagon pulled by six horses, the triple wagon-boxes piled high under snow-blanketed tarps. Gordon counted a dozen wagons, and more might be ahead. He could see no escort of men on horseback.

There were at least two men on each wagon, however, and the total would add up to a formidable force.

Inevitably, the pursuers had been seen. At sight of them, sudden panic seemed to develop among the fugitives. The wagons had topped a long, easy rise. Now, ahead for as far as could be seen, the road dropped, gradually but surely. With that advantage, the drivers whipped up their horses, sending the lumbering wagons into a swaying, jolting race.

'They're scared!' Drake gritted from beside Gordon. 'And they've a right to be!'

Only panic, or some similar emotion, could have persuaded the drivers that such an effort would be of any avail, though for the first half-mile, the teams, aided by the down-grade, maintained their distance. Then the riders on horseback commenced to narrow the gap, and after that it closed swiftly. Gordon lifted his gun and fired a couple of shots in the air as a signal to halt.

Reluctantly, the others obeyed, and the wagons were standing in a long, strung-out line as they came up, the heavy breath of the draft horses like fog upon the air. Somewhat to his surprise, Gordon did not recognize any of the drivers, nor were they making any show of resistance.

'What's all this about?' one demanded. 'What you stoppin' us for?'

'You know very well what we're stoppin' you for!' Lomax snapped. 'You with loads of stolen meat!'

108

The other man's eyebrows raised.

'Stolen meat? That'a serious charge to make—and you'd better be able to back it up, mister!'

'We'll back it up, all right,' Lomax growled. 'We're going to have a look under those tarps. And don't try to stop us!'

The driver shrugged.

'Looks like you can have your way, seeing the size of your crew,' he conceded. 'Have a look if you want. We've nothing to hide. This is Getchell's Freight—and we're hauling on contract.'

Gordon knew about Getchell. He had commenced hauling with a pair of run-down wagons and some equally worn-out horses, at the time when the camp had begun operations. As the camp had prospered, so had he, bringing in supplies and taking out ore. Now, apparently, he owned this whole string of wagons. The possibility that O'Dion might be the real owner of the freight outfit had not occurred to Gordon until then.

Such an established business was a good cover for the present job. Again he had the nagging feeling that they had been outwitted, outmatched, but there was nothing for it but to go through with what they'd started. Some of the crew were loosening ropes, throwing back the tarps.

In part, they saw what they had expected to see—the close-piled, frozen carcasses of butchered calves. Regarding that, there could be no question. There had been no time to cut them up, and they were impossible to disguise.

At that point the evidence faltered. Clearly O'Dion had foreseen the possibility of discovery. The calves had been skinned, and the telltale hides, with their incriminating brands, were no longer on them, nor were any to be seen.

The driver regarded them sardonically.

'Satisfied?' he asked. 'You got any proof that those chunks of meat belong to you?'

'Take a look all along the line,' Gordon instructed, disregarding him. But he knew, by the bland attitude of the transport men, that it was hopeless. That was soon confirmed. There were no hides in any of the wagons.

Again, the thing was unbelievable. They had followed closely after the wagons, yet somewhere along the way they had been spoofed, fooled. Without evidence they could do nothing, and they'd be a laughing-stock as well.

CHAPTER ELEVEN

So many hides, even those of calves, would take up a lot of room, filling more than one wagon. With such brands burned into the skin, they were tangible evidence, the sort which could not readily be disposed of. Had they been flung over the side, even among deep drifts, they would be found. The hungrily questing coyotes, with noses attuned to the smell of meat, would make sure of that. It was to make certain that such proof was not found that O'Dion was going to extreme lengths.

Gordon had the bitter conviction that he was being cleverly fooled. Somewhere along the line, they had overlooked something.

The answer hit him with the force of a blast of the blizzard, and he pulled his horse half-around, then checked the gesture. If he was right, there was no hurry. In this situation, he couldn't afford either to tip or overplay his hand.

'I'm putting in a claim before these men as witnesses,' he announced. 'All of this meat is from stolen cattle, and it belongs to Slash Y. Go ahead and deliver it if you like, but I warn you that in the end you'll have to pay for it.'

The driver of the first wagon shrugged.

'Mister, you produce some proof to back up your words, and that'll be a different matter. Till you do, it's a case of put up or shut up! As for us, we're going on.'

There was no way to stop them, short of a fight, and the taunting note in his voice, as well as the look on other faces, showed that they hoped for just that. They were playing for delay. Gordon remounted and turned back. After an uncertain moment, the other Slash riders followed.

'What now?' Lomax demanded. 'You got a new notion?'

'I sure have,' Gordon agreed. 'They had a piece of luck, that we overtook them just where we did, though the chances are that they held back till they saw us coming, to make sure that we'd come up with them at that particular place—where they could act scared and make a show of running.'

'You mean they wanted us to chase them?'

'What else? And they worked it so that we accommodated them, and ran right past a side-road that turns off toward New Cheyenne. As I recall, the turn-off is near the top of the hill.'

Drake's uncertain face lightened.

'Sure, that must be it. The hide wagons were ahead and made the turn—then the others waited to lure us past, so that we wouldn't notice!'

'That just about has to be the way of it. We'll take a short cut and catch up with the others.'

'And when we do, they'll have to pay for that meat, like you told them.' Drake grinned. 'I want to be in on presentin' that bill!'

Wind and storm had all but obliterated the

sign at the turn-off, but a quarter of a mile farther along the new route, where the wind brushed lightly, the trail was clear and easy to follow. It was plain that the wagons with the hides were well ahead, the drivers pushing their teams at top speed to reach their destination.

'They'll likely take them straight to Barclay's,' Gordon said.

Barclay's was a hide and fur house, whose reputation had spread widely if not favorably. Barclay was not averse to dealing in honest produce, but it was an open secret that he preferred questionable consignments, which frequently offered greater opportunities for profit.

New Cheyenne owed its existence largely to the existence of the mining and lumbering camp, and was not much older. It had sprung up, toad-stool fashion, as a supply base for the camps. Since it served a real need, with a big spread of country on every side, its growth had been rapid. In the last year it had out-distanced the older community of Long Rain, which was also the county seat. Besides Barclay's it boasted several more or less solid businesses.

Gordon halted again, and the others grouped around him.

'A couple of us will go on,' he explained. 'Those wagons will reach New Cheyenne ahead of us, and if we all rode in, the whole town would turn out to stop us. So the best way will be to slip in, have a look around, and discover the evidence, then act. The rest of you get back to the ranch and keep an eye on things. Sam and I will do the snooping.'

Drake was grinning in anticipation as they went on.

'I suppose you know who Barclay is?' he suggested.

'All I know is what I've heard,' Gordon confessed. 'They say he'll accept a cargo of misbranded hides and no questions asked—if the price is right. But I've never been over this way before.'

'Me neither—but I've heard aplenty. In this case, they'll fix the price between them—O'Dion, Lem Harder and Barclay. Barclay's half-brother to the sheriff.'

That explained such points as had been obscure. It explained why Barclay could go unmolested, despite his conducting of a shady business. It explained why O'Dion was sending the hides to him. Once they had been unloaded and stored inside the big warehouse, it would be difficult to get a look at them. They would then be shipped out, hidden among bundles of legitimate cargo.

Everyone knew what went on, but obtaining proof was something else. It was highly effective to have the weight of the law, or what passed for law in that country, on your side.

'How we going to work it?' Drake asked. 'I've heard about Barclay's. They say his warehouse is a long building, with iron bars on the windows and padlocks on the doors; not easy to get into or out of.'

'And whoever's in charge would be suspicious of strangers,' Gordon observed. 'They'd probably ask for credentials.'

'And ours wouldn't suit—'less they're stamped by Colonel Colt. But if that's what they require—' He shrugged and grinned again.

'We'll have to wait and see what comes up,' Gordon responded. One way or another, he intended to have a look at the evidence. Properly presented, it might be enough to defeat O'Dion, without the need for a bloody showdown.

As the excitement of the new venture wore off, the cold crept back, chilling them from head to foot. A couple of times they dismounted, leading their horses, to warm themselves, but that made for slow going and helped only a little. Drake's voice was wistful.

'You think maybe we could risk getting a bite to eat when we get there?' he asked. 'And can we have a chance to thaw out?'

'We'll sure enough take the chance,' Gordon agreed. He had an idea that the temperature had dropped below zero, and it was still plummeting. The day had been long, and, hastened by clouds and the relentless

115

storm, night would come soon after they reached the town. They would have to eat and get warm. That was a bare minimum for existence.

New Cheyenne was a long way from Long Rain, a country apart. Even so, some of its inhabitants might recognize one or both of them, in which case their mission would be easily guessed. The chance of success would be enhanced if such recognition could be avoided.

They could see only an outline of the town as they approached. Darkness was already at hand, with lights springing up here and there, like faint candles against the vastness of the winter night. The snow swirled and drifted.

The first building, set well apart from its neighbors, was long and low, and a couple of big wagons stood alongside. The teams had been unhitched, the cargo unloaded. Despite the bitter cold, odors drifted out, making clear that this was the hide warehouse.

It was easy to make a circle, unobserved, with no one around. The heavy door was padlocked.

The next building was a livery stable, and here a lantern gave a feeble glow. They turned in, the horses stumbling with weariness. The stable boy, a lanky youth with unkempt hair whose hue matched the hay he forked, displayed no interest in them or the brands on the horses.

116

He was in the midst of forking hay to them when a clamor sounded outside, and he dropped the fork and rushed eagerly to the door. Voices exclaimed in relief or complaint, some of them feminine. It was apparent that the stage had arrived, delayed well beyond its usual schedule by the difficult weather. At least three heavily bundled figures climbed stiffly down from the box, while from inside was debouched a cargo of humanity, which appeared to have been packed as tightly as hides, once they were bailed for shipment.

Watching from the background, Gordon and Drake marveled that so many people had managed to crowd their way in. There were more than a dozen in all, and one man explained that a second stage had broken down, compelling them all to take the one. They were a theatrical company, a traveling road company who were scheduled to put on a show that same evening, at the opera house.

Those were magic words, testimony to the growth and affluence of New Cheyenne. It had had an opera house for almost a year. Because of that, O'Dion had gotten the notion of establishing a theatre in Long Rain, turning O'Rourke's Saloon into the Grand Theatre. This same road company would be going on to Long Rain after their engagement here.

The passengers lost no time in trooping off toward the main part of town, anxious to get supper and to refresh themselves before it was time to put on the play. Most of them were laden with baggage and stage props as the storm swallowed them.

The driver of the stage was pressed into service to help transport some of the gear, once a huge pile of it was unlashed and taken down from the rear of the stage. That left the stable-boy to handle the six horses alone.

Gordon and Drake moved to assist him. The stolid youngster was now eager and voluble. Here was a subject dear to his heart.

'Yeah, they're the thee-atrical company,' he confirmed. 'I was sure gettin' worried that they wouldn't make it tonight, and if they hadn't, a lot of folks would have been mighty disappointed. They're puttin' on a three-act play, "Our American Cousin." That's the one President Lincoln was watchin' when he was shot.'

He pointed to a poster tacked to the wall, visible in the light from a hanging lantern. The style was flamboyant, the poster a yellow sheet which was already beginning to fade and discolor.

'Read it,' the boy urged. 'Ain't that something, now? Read it out loud,' he added. 'I sure like to hear it.'

Rightly deducing that he was unable to read for himself, Gordon complied.

The Renowned
Great Lakes and Seaboard Players
Under the Direction of
Mr. Scott Glosson
Present
OUR AMERICAN COUSIN

Following was the cast, including such characters as Georgina Mountchessington, Captain DeBoots and Lord Dundreary. The boy repeated the names, rolling them off his tongue with gusto.

'I sure aim to see that,' he asserted.

'You know, I wouldn't mind seein' it myself,' Drake confessed, and sighed wistfully.

'It would be nice,' Gordon agreed, though he knew that it would be out of the question. They went outside, conscious anew of the bite of cold, and set off in the tracks of the theatrical company. Drake stumbled, almost falling, then plucked from the snow the object against which he had stubbed his toe. It was a carpetbag.

'I'll bet those folks dropped this,' he observed. 'They were so loaded down with stuff they wouldn't have noticed. Maybe we should give it to them.'

'Let's have a look,' Gordon suggested. The bag was partly open, some of the contents on the verge of spilling. Excitement gripped him as he looked closer. These were theatrical props—sets of false whiskers, as well as other articles about whose use he was uncertain.

'We'll leave the bag where they'll find it,' he decided. 'But let's follow the pattern of some others in this town and engage in a bit of petty larceny.' He thrust a generous mustache into Drake's hand. 'It seems to be ready to stick on, just by pressing it down. I'll take this set of whiskers.'

The beard was full and black, and served pretty well to hide his face, completely altering his appearance. Drake stared, dumbfounded, in the faintly reflected light from a store window, then backed away.

'If I didn't know who you were, I'd sure be scared to meet you on a night like this,' he asserted. 'You look like a desperado.'

'You're quite a character yourself, with that mustache,' Gordon assured him. Again, faint light shone through a frosted window, and the sign as well as the fragrance indicated that this was a restaurant. The unmistakable voice of one of the actors reached them.

'Food, my good fellow, food is what we require. Sustenance for the bodily man, hot, and in plenitude. What it shall be we leave to you, only let it be your best.'

Gordon placed the carpet bag on the steps.

'They'll find this, all right—and I hope our appropriations won't leave them short. We'll have to pick some other place to eat, for they might recognize our whiskers.'

They found another restaurant across the

street; it was virtually deserted. Everyone who could was clustering in the other, if not to patronize it, then to gaze in awe-struck admiration at these beings from another world, who were bringing not only entertainment but culture to the community. Some might be perfectly willing to share in the profits from such mundane enterprises as the hide house, but for this evening at least, they were anxious to forget such things.

'Sure a piece of luck, them hittin' town and putting on the show tonight,' Drake observed. 'Nobody'll have any time or interest for anything else.'

As though his words had summoned them, another pair of customers entered, seating themselves at another table. They gave only a cursory glance at the two already there, then began to confer, low-toned. It was as he was starting on his pie that Gordon caught a phrase:

'—couldn't be better, a night like this, with everybody headin' for that playhouse. I'll show you what we've got in the warehouse. Mighty fine shipment came in today.'

CHAPTER TWELVE

Gordon paid for the meal, taking time to engage the waiter in conversation, to inquire about obtaining tickets for the show. Having implanted the idea that the theatre was their destination, they went back outside. It was full dark now, as unpleasant a night as could well be imagined.

Farther up the street, a lantern burned fitfully, buffeted but not quite blown out by the gusts of wind. It marked the path to the opera house. Despite the inclement weather, people were already streaming in, making certain of a place to view this opening performance of the season.

'They tell me that the play is quite a show, an excellent comedy,' Gordon commented, 'though in everyone's mind now it is associated with tragedy. Too bad we can't see it.'

'Yeah, but for a choice, I'd rather see the inside of that hide house,' Drake grunted. 'Here they come.'

The other two diners emerged, then set off toward the warehouse and were immediately swallowed in the darkness. Following, it was unnecessary to take precautions, just as it was impossible to see those who went before. But they had only to follow the beaten road to reach the hide house.

The big padlock hung open, and they pushed open the door and let themselves in. Halfway down the length of the long room, a lantern bobbed, the two men moving between hides stacked higher than their heads. Some were dry, already baled, ready for shipping out. Others, clearly the calfskins, were frozen together in great piles.

The two were discussing these. It appeared that the one man was a hide buyer, representing some outside company. The man who was showing him around was Barclay.

'Those fresh brands are bad business,' the buyer protested. 'If anybody was to get a look at them, they're evidence. And the condition they're in, the brands make for a lot of wastage. Every one will have to be cut out, and that chunk of skin burned.'

'Which I'm taking into account,' Barclay reminded him somewhat sharply. 'I'm making you a mighty good price on the lot.'

'Not good enough, considering. I don't mind a few bad hides scattered here and there among a lot of bales. That's normal. But all these—I've never seen anything like it. Somebody was takin' a mighty big chance.'

'If it's taking a chance that worries you, forget it. Getchell's wagons hauled them here, and Getchell will haul them on to Salt Lake and turn them over to you there.'

'Well, if I take delivery there, that's different. But Getchell must be crazy to take such chances.'

'I tell you he takes none. The sheriff is my half-brother; Getchell is my cousin. And it's Curt O'Dion who is selling these skins.

O'Dion owns half this country—and it won't be long till he has the rest of it.'

'Includin' the men in it, and the law, eh? Well, that puts a different face on the matter. I'll take delivery at Salt Lake, and pay on delivery.'

Barclay's head-shake caused the lantern to bob.

'Not good enough. You'll pay half down, now, same as on other deals, same as we agreed on. If you don't trust me, I don't trust you that far, either—not with a cargo like this.'

The conversation was highly interesting, but this seemed a good time to take over. The pair stared with widening eyes as the other diners stepped from the gloom, with guns aimed.

'Sorry to interrupt such a high-minded deal as you're cooking up,' Gordon observed blandly. 'But you do engage in a chancy business. Get their guns, Sam.'

The hide buyer was quaking, and he offered no resistance. Barclay sought to bluster, mouthing threats, and when those had no effect, he sought to bribe them. Drake worked silently, disarming them; then, using a piece of rope which was conveniently at hand, he sliced it into lengths and tied them hand and foot.

Such grim precision, all in silence, was having its effect. Barclay was as jittery as his companion.

'What you going to do?' he demanded. 'You can't just leave us here—that's murder. We'll freeze.'

'Hardly that.' Gordon shrugged. 'But lie on the floor, and we'll throw some skins over you, to keep you warm.' As they were half-shoved, half-eased into place by Drake, he selected a dry cowhide and spread it over them.

They took a couple of the calfskins with the fresh Quirt brands, forced to pull and pry to get them loose, for the green, frozen hides were hard to handle. Then, deaf to the pleas of their captives, they went out, snapping the padlock in place.

'They'll work loose, but they'll probably have to spend the night there,' Gordon observed. 'With everybody at the opera house, and the storm on top of that, I doubt that they can make themselves heard.'

Except for horses, the stable was empty. The stable boy had slipped away as planned. They selected a fresh pair of horses from those in the stalls, and Gordon scribbled a note on the back of the theatre poster, tearing it loose for the purpose. He explained that they were leaving their own animals as evidence of good faith and would return the others within a few days.

'Perhaps they won't like it, but like us, they won't have much choice,' he granted, and turned his cayuse into the storm.

It was a punishing ride. Keeping to the road was largely a matter of instinct on the part of the horses, who went reluctantly. Like himself, Drake possessed an instinct for going straight even under adverse conditions. Both of them were reasonably confident that they were keeping in the right direction.

At intervals they walked, leading the horses, warming themselves and giving the animals a breather. Finally, almost numb with cold, Gordon risked a swing, leaving the road, and Drake roused from a long silence to grunt a question.

'What's up? Where we headin'?'

'Slash,' Gordon explained. 'The house ought to be off there about a mile.'

Drake sighed in relief.

'That close? I thought we'd keep on to Long Rain.'

'I doubt if we could make it,' Gordon said frankly. 'I'm about at the end of my rope, and so are the horses. We'll get some rest and food before we go on.'

'Sure suits me. I didn't think I could keep going,' Drake confessed. 'But if you kept moving, I figured I'd tag along.'

Absently, Gordon fingered the icicles which had formed on mustache and whiskers from his icy breath. He sensed that the storm was finally slackening, the snow ebbing, the wind dying. There was a lightening in the cloud wrack overhead, and in that faint illumination he made out the dark cluster of ranch buildings.

They got the horses into the barn, tugging off saddles by feel and instinct, their fingers too numb to strike a match or make a light. Keeping together, they stumbled across to the bunk house and tugged open the door. Gordon crashed against some obstacle, and a startled voice demanded to know who was there.

'Us—Drake and Gordon,' he mumbled, and drew in a long breath of the warmer, but still chill air. There was another grunt of surprise; then others of the crew came tumbling from their bunks, to light a lamp, then to build a fire in the stove, at the same time exclaiming in pity and disbelief.

'But you ain't Gordon,' one man protested. 'You cain't be—even if you do sound like him.'

Gordon caught a glimpse of himself in the mirror on the wall, and stared incredulously. He had forgotten all about the heavy set of false whiskers, too preoccupied with other matters to remember. They were still in place, probably having shielded his face from some of the bitter cold during the ride. They accounted for the clustering icicles on mustache and beard.

He clawed these loose as they commenced to loosen in the warmth of the room, sending them rattling to the floor, then pulled off the whiskers. He accepted a drink from a proffered bottle, a long, deep potion which barely warmed his throat. One man was tugging off his boots, while another performed the same service for Drake. He'd intended to ask questions as to what had taken place during their absence, but the next thing he knew he was in his bunk and tumbling into sweet oblivion.

It was daylight when he awoke, to discover that he had slept the clock around. Outside, the clouds still shut away the sun, the world looking white and cheerless. His discovery that it was past noon shocked him fully awake. He'd had no intention of sleeping so long.

At the ranch itself there had been no trouble. But the other members of the crew, who had ridden with him the day before, and who had been sent back under Lomax, had not been seen.

He wondered about them uneasily, though it was probable that they had tired of the ride in such bitter weather, and had sought shelter, also sleeping late.

By now, the veal meat would be on the tables at the construction camp, and the branded hides might be on their way to Salt Lake, consigned along with other skins, with a faked bill of sale. Thus the evidence would soon vanish.

Drake roused, blinked and yawned as Gordon shook him, then tumbled reluctantly from the bunk.

'Man, I never slept like that before in my life,' he confessed, and eyed the blankets wistfully. 'And I wouldn't mind crawlin' back in for another round of the same!'

'It sounds like a great idea,' Gordon conceded. 'But how about something to eat? Then we still have to finish our ride.'

'Now you mention food, I believe I could do with a bite or so—about the size bites a starvin' grizzly would grab off.' Drake grinned. They ate; then Gordon took time to shave. Feeling halfway himself again, he crossed to the house.

Mary McKay was frankly glad to see him. Her face betrayed the anxiety she had felt.

'I was certainly relieved this morning when I heard that you were back, though they said that you were just about all in when you returned late last night. We all worried, of course, with such bad weather on top of all the rest.'

'I'm going to take that worry as being more or less personal,' Gordon observed. 'Which gives me a chance to ask a question that I've been wondering about. The more I've thought it over, the more it seems to me that that meeting at Selway's Restaurant the other evening must have been set up by somebody—planned to stir up trouble. What do you know about it?'

'Not much, but I think you're probably right,' Mary agreed. A trace of color flowed in her pale cheeks and forehead. 'I never did get it quite straight, but Driscoll dropped some remarks which make me think you are right. Someone had been taunting him, and others of our crew, about being afraid of Quirt, and standing aside for them on certain days, as though Quirt had any better right to a place to eat than the Slash. Of course such talk was foolish, and only designed to cause trouble—but it worked.'

'It sure did. I knew there must have been some reason why Slash would violate the truce the way it did.'

'Well, a part of the reason—' Her color was higher now, but she met his eyes steadily. 'Part was talk, that you had been seeing me on the sly—that you were interested in a girl who would inherit a big slice of a big ranch. I got that much out of Driscoll afterward. Of course there was no truth in any of it, but it served its purpose. He was always hot-headed and impulsive.'

The explanation cleared up certain points, and definitely proved that the whole scheme had been contrived, carefully planned. As far as Slash Y was concerned, the purpose was readily understandable. But why had he been picked as the goat? The nagging question was still unanswered, but somehow it had a big part in the total sum of events. For he had been sent into town by O'Dion himself, on what had turned out to be a completely trifling errand; sent in alone, to get into trouble, perhaps to die.

CHAPTER THIRTEEN

Riding toward Long Rain, Gordon was preoccupied. Sam Drake offered a tentative remark or so concerning the improving weather, then, finding that he received no answer, lapsed into silence. The pair of calfskins were tied behind Drake's saddle, evidence which could be shown to the law. But Abe McKay's eyebrows had lifted skeptically, and Gordon, viewing matters in the cold light of day, felt almost as skeptical. Where would be the profit in forcing evidence upon a man who was determined not to look at it?

Even so, it had to be tried. The law must be given a chance to handle the situation if it would. Not until legal recourse had been attempted could he justify turning to Judge Colt for a decision, with the writing in red.

The short winter day was waning as they reached the town. There would be time enough to visit the sheriff's office and show the evidence, and that was about all. By now,

Gordon's mood was almost as stark as the day. Maybe it had been a fatal mistake to play the game as he had. A showdown, however heavy the odds, would still have given them a fighting chance. But with a law which abetted and protected the lawless—

A shrill voice, almost piping, roused him from his reverie. Someone had called from the snow-packed sidewalk. Eli Jenkins, postmaster, bulked formidably, clad in a heavy cap and buffalo coat, barely recognized as the slight, meek little man who usually hovered behind his cubbyhole and peered timidly out through the wicket. Gordon pulled up.

'Did you want to see me, Mr. Jenkins?' he asked.

'I fear so, sir—indeed, I believe so. Could I have a few words with you, Mr. Gordon?'

'No reason why not,' Gordon agreed, surprised. When in town, he usually called at the post office for Quirt mail, and so was casually acquainted with the postmaster. Rarely, if ever, had they exchanged more than the time of day, just as there was seldom any mail for himself.

'Look after the horses,' he instructed Drake. 'I'll join you at the stable.' He dismounted to join the bundled figure on the sidewalk. 'What is it?'

'Let's step inside the post office,' Jenkins suggested. 'It'll be warmer there.'

Gordon followed willingly. The warmth was welcome after the ride into town. A cherry-red heater gulped hungrily at a split log; then Jenkins divested himself of the heavy coat, tugged off the fur cap, and became again his usual meek self. He peered uncertainly, as if disliking the question he had to ask.

'I—something set me to wondering,' he confessed. 'Perhaps a chain of incidents. But you—I presume that you received your letter all right, the other day?'

'Letter? What letter?' Gordon asked. 'I haven't had a letter, or any piece of mail, for going on a year now. I never write, and nobody writes to me.'

Jenkins made a small clucking noise. 'Dear me,' he protested. 'Are you telling me that your employer, Mr. O'Dion, failed to give you the registered letter which came for you? He signed for it—and since he was your employer, to say nothing of being Mr. O'Dion, I assumed—quite naturally—that there would be no question as to its delivery. Of course, I should have had you sign for it yourself. Oh, dear me!'

'When was this?' Gordon asked. 'I've had no letter, or any word about one.'

'Incredible. I can't understand such forgetfulness on the part of Mr. O'Dion. It was ten days, possibly a couple of weeks ago, that a letter came, addressed to you. I remember quite distinctly that it was from Kentucky—a registered letter. I assumed—mistakenly, it now appears—'

'Kentucky? You wouldn't remember the return address, or the town it was from?'

'Yes, I recall the point of mailing quite well. It was Frankfort. Also, the envelope had been torn in transit. The enclosure was not too well protected, as I pointed out to Mr. O'Dion—'

'I used to have an uncle who lived in Frankfort,' Gordon commented thoughtfully. 'I never saw him but once in my life, and then I was too small to remember. I'd supposed he must have died years ago.'

'As to that, of course, I cannot say, but I blame myself—most severely—for carelessness, for dereliction of duty, in regard to your letter. It must have been important; else it would not have been registered. And I—it has come to my ears that you are no longer employed at the Quirt—'

'No, I'm not,' Gordon agreed. On the face of it, he couldn't see how the receipt of such a letter could be very important, though the timing and the fact that O'Dion had not turned it over to him, or mentioned it in any way, might be significant. If the envelope had been torn, O'Dion might have had a look at what it contained. Meanwhile, the day was running out, and so was time.

The door opened, letting in a swirl of air

which gusted frostily across the room, and a bundled figure thrust a small package toward the postmaster.

'Here's the mail,' he explained. 'That's all there was this time. Not a single letter or paper—that must have got held up somewhere and missed the stage. Just this one package. Registered mail. Sign for it, will you?'

Jenkins did so, moving mechanically, peering somewhat nearsightedly at the package. His head jerked violently and he looked again. Then, as the door closed behind the messenger, he thrust it at Gordon.

'This is for you,' he said heavily. 'From the same place—Frankfort, Kentucky. You sign this time, and I'm putting it into your own hands.'

Surprised, but agreeable, Gordon signed, studying the packet a moment. He thrust it into a pocket, and with Jenkins' apologies for the earlier error still sounding in his ears, returned to the street.

Drake was waiting at the livery stable. There, in the shelter of a stall, Gordon ripped open the package, then stared in increasing astonishment, along with a glimmer of understanding.

The package contained a thick sheaf of money. There were hundred-dollar bills, gleaming with newness, carefully wrapped. A hasty count indicated the amount to be

135

twenty thousand dollars. Drake blinked in astonishment.

'What's going on?' he asked. 'Have you fallen heir to a fortune or something?'

'It looks like that—or something, sure enough,' Gordon agreed. The letter had probably contained an explanation and necessary information; he could begin to fit certain obvious facts into an answer.

As far as he knew, his uncle had been his only living relative, so, by the same token, he was probably his uncle's sole heir. He'd never known or even wondered as to whether or not this relative had any property, or thought of himself in connection with it. It was surprising that an uncle who had never written should have kept track of a nephew sufficiently to know his whereabouts.

Yet he must have done so, and now the estate, in cash, had been sent to him. Thinking back, he recalled that his uncle had been mentioned as a man of strong opinions and prejudices, one of which had been his great distrust of banks. He had never kept any money in them. It would have been natural for him to instruct whoever was delegated the task of settling up his estate to send the money in cash.

Ironically, the administrator must have secured new money from a bank!

Quite clearly, the letter, which had arrived ahead of the money, must have explained

136

these details and said that the cash was coming. When O'Dion had learned that one of his crew was to receive such a sum of money, he'd kept the information to himself, then set about scheming to get hold of it. In view of his other activities, that was not surprising. Twenty thousand dollars would be a juicy windfall.

It might well be that that particular piece of information had helped trigger other events, including the timing of the attack against Slash. There had been those stories carefully planted in the ears of Driscoll McKay and others of the Slash Y; the sending him to town, alone, on that particular day. Events were clear enough now. He was not called Brick for nothing; he had red hair and a temper to match. If his propensity for trouble should lead him into more of it than he could handle, on the eve of the arrival of the money, O'Dion, as his employer, would know to handle all that.

The scheme hadn't worked entirely according to plan, especially since the money had been turned over to him now. But it explained a lot, all of which fitted into the larger ambitions of O'Dion.

Gordon hesitated, then shoved the package into his saddle-bags. Drake had the other package containing the frozen hides.

'Don't mention anything about this money to anybody,' Gordon cautioned. 'Let's go make our call on the sheriff.'

Drake shrugged, but contained his curiosity as they swung down the street. The clouds were showing signs of breaking, and it would probably be a colder night than ever, but with sunshine on the morrow. Now, early though the hour was, dusk was closing over the town.

The stone pile of the two-story courthouse was off at one side, a few pale blobs of light gleaming murkily through windows heavy with frost. They headed for the sheriff's office, connected with the jail a block away. A light there betokened that someone was still around.

There another red-hot stove made the room over-warm. Lem Harder was seated, boots on his desk, chin on his chest. His chin jerked and the boots made a thump on the floor as he swung guiltily at the opening of the door. His face went blank as he recognized Gordon, then smoothed to its usual, faintly oily composure, though he checked his start toward rising.

'You want something?' he asked gruffly.

'We've something to show you,' Drake explained and, cutting the cord which held the rolled-up skins in position, struggled to unroll them. Holding them close to the stove, he gradually succeeded, as the heat thawed the ice. The sheriff was on his feet now, watching sharply, his face still expressionless.

Drake spread the evidence on the floor.

'We thought you should see this,' Gordon explained. 'Quirt stole the entire calf crop of Slash Y the other day—ran off cows and their calves alike, then branded the calves with the Quirt. We went across there, Slash Y's whole crew, and found them with their mothers, all Slash Y cows. We got them back, but Quirt was alarmed by then, and that night they moved in, butchered the calves, and shipped out the meat and the skins. We found the meat en route to the big construction camp, and the hides in Barclay's hide house at New Cheyenne. We brought a couple of them to show you.'

The sheriff listened, with varying shades of expression, then shook his head unbelievingly.

'Do you expect me to believe a wild yarn like that,' he asked, 'or any part of it?'

'Here's proof,' Gordon pointed out grimly. 'And we've plenty of witnesses—the whole Slash Y crew.'

Challenged by such a solid argument, Harder veered to a new tack. 'I'd heard that you'd turned renegade from Quirt,' he observed bitingly. 'But I didn't suppose that anyone would go quite this far.'

'Let's leave your opinions and suppositions out of it,' Gordon suggested. 'You're the sheriff, so we've come to you. We represent Slash Y, and this is a case of rustling on a wholesale scale. We want you to do something about it.'

'You say you found those skins in the hide warehouse at New Cheyenne? How did you get hold of them?'

'We went in, had a look around, then helped ourselves to some of the evidence, to show you. The whole calf crop of Slash was there, all branded with the Quirt.'

Harder shrugged.

'You mean you found hides branded with Quirt. That is no proof that the rustling wasn't against Quirt—though that's what the evidence would seem to indicate.'

'We told you where they came from. We followed the hide wagons all the way from where the calves were butchered on Slash Y, and we have plenty of witnesses.'

'Witnesses?' The sheriff was shaken, searching for a way out of this dilemma. The last thing that he wanted to do was to enforce the law against his real employer, O'Dion, or against his cousin or brother-in-law, all of whom were so deeply involved. Yet as sheriff, he had obligations not readily shrugged aside.

'If you expect me to believe any part of so wild a story, you'll have to make it credible,' he said carefully. 'I've been in Barclay's hide house, so I know what it's like. He keeps it locked, except for people who had legitimate business there. I don't for a minute believe that he'd have let you in, under the circumstances—or that he'd let you out again, with evidence such as that, if what you say is true. In that case, such evidence could land him in trouble up to his neck.'

'We got in,' Gordon reminded, 'and had our look. And we've brought the evidence. Now, this isn't a matter for you to please yourself about. We're speaking as citizens, as representatives of Slash Y. What I've told you, we make as a charge against Quirt—stealing Slash cows and calves, misbranding them, then slaughtering the calves. We want action, and fast, to stop those skins from being shipped out of the country. We want the evidence impounded for a jury to look at.'

Harder hesitated, chewing his lip. He was fairly caught, and he knew it. If he refused, and the story got abroad, then was confirmed, he'd be through as sheriff; worse than that, he'd be lucky to get out of the county without being tarred and feathered.

On the other hand, he owed his job to O'Dion, and some of his relatives were implicated; Gordon suspected that Harder also had a share in the business, so he had to protect them in every way possible, even to further subversion of the law—which was the reason he had been put in as sheriff in the first place.

He swung in sudden decision, nodding.

'Maybe you've got a case,' he

141

acknowledged. 'I never heard a crazier-sounding story in my life, but if you take the necessary legal steps, I'll do my part. What you want is for me to go to New Cheyenne and impound those hides?'

'That's a first step.'

'That's the second step,' the sheriff contradicted. 'The first is for you to go to the judge and get a warrant to search that warehouse, one which will authorize me to seize and impound the evidence if found. I can't do such a thing merely on your say-so. Get that; then I'll ride.'

'We'll get it.' Gordon was shrugging back into his heavy coat. Drake gathered up the hides. 'Get ready to ride!'

CHAPTER FOURTEEN

For all his show of confidence, Gordon was far from certain if they would get far. Night was closing over the town as they headed for the courthouse, though it was not yet so dark but what their breath steamed about their faces, while boots crunched like sled runners in the snow. Harder would go only as far and fast as he was compelled.

The hides might already be beyond reach; suddenly it seemed like a hopeless task. But they were too deeply involved for any other course. This must be played to the end.

The courthouse corridors were dimly lit, dank and echoing. A clerk appeared suddenly from the shadows to halt them short of the judge's chambers. He listened doubtfully to their request to see the judge at once.

'Well, I don't know about that,' he hedged. 'It's closing time, and past. You'd better come back tomorrow.'

'Tomorrow will be too late,' Gordon protested. 'This is urgent business, and we want to see him now—at once!'

'Well, I'll tell him that you're here,' the clerk agreed, and withdrew. He was gone a long while, during which they could only wait and fume. Finally he returned, to announce that the judge would see them.

Judge Uland was tall and thin, and his habit of dressing always in black, coupled with a beak of a nose under eyebrows like miniature mustaches, gave him the appearace of a bird of prey. Before his elevation to the bench, he had enjoyed a dubious reputation as a lawyer, so much so that even the backing of Quirt had barely gotten him elected. Like the sheriff, he did not forget to whom he owed his elevation. He peered forbiddingly from behind his desk, scowling at the hides outspread on the floor.

'You tell a somewhat incredible story,' he pronounced. 'However, for the moment, the matter of credibility is secondary. Just exactly

143

how did you get hold of these—of this evidence?'

Not giving time for a reply, he leaned across his desk to waggle a finger in their faces, then altered the gesture to a snap of the fingers. At that manifest signal, the rear door to the office oepned and the sheriff entered.

'On that point you have been evasive, both with me and with Sheriff Harder,' Uland thundered. 'That attitude is easily understandable, since the truth would implicate you. It is clearly evident that you obtained these skins by breaking and entering, with felonious intent. Need I remind you that such conduct is a crime of a most serious order? Accordingly, I hereby instruct the sheriff to place you under arrest and to hold you in close custody, while this affair is sifted and investigated and the truth arrived at.'

He should have expected something of the sort, Gordon realized bitterly. He'd forced Quirt and its henchmen into a position where their backs were against the wall. In that situation, they would go to any lengths.

When he attempted to protest, the judge overrode him with a roar.

'This court will permit no quibbling,' he thundered, 'particularly in view of the stories which have come to my ear concerning the murder of Driscoll McKay—above whose dead body you were discovered! Lock them up, Sheriff.'

It was a bitter moment as the sheriff thrust them triumphantly into a cell, not troubling to hide his elation. Clearly he had scuttled across to the courtroom by the back way, beating them there, gaining the ear of the judge and apprising him of the seriousness of the situation. While they had been kept waiting, the two had planned a course of action.

Beyond question, their intent was to keep them locked up, at least long enough for the evidence to be transported out of the territory, and until O'Dion had tidied up his affairs. It would require only a little more to place Slash in a position where it could no longer fight back and, deprived of leadership, O'Dion would move ruthlessly against the ranch. His blunder had lain in trying to fight back within the law, seeking to avoid a bloody range war. These men didn't play by such rules.

To his demand that they be allowed to see a lawyer, Harder shrugged. Clearly, he would find reasons for not getting word to a lawyer that evening.

Both prisoners were doubly surprised when, within half an hour, Larry Vick came into the jail, accompanied by a grumpy sheriff. Vick was comparatively new in the territory, still a tenderfoot by most standards. But he was a lawyer, and already he had demonstrated that he was not only competent but hard to bluff. He explained why he was there.

'It appears that Miss McKay and her father were rather dubious as to how you might make out, so they followed you right to town,' he said. 'They got here just in time to find that you had been arrested, so they have hired me to look after your interests. Let's hear your story; then I'll go to the judge and try to arrange for bail.'

He listened, with no appearance of surprise, asking a few clarifying questions, then set out as promised. Hopefully they waited, and when he returned, the look on his face told that the news was bad.

'Sure, he agreed to grant bail,' Vick reported bitterly. 'Ten thousand dollars, cash money, for Drake—and as much more for you, Gordon, on the charge of breaking and entering, with an added fifteen thousand in your case, on suspicion of murder. I attempted to persuade him to adopt a more reasonable attitude—' He smiled wryly. 'In fact, I'm afraid I almost lost my temper. His Honor—I use the term loosely—soaked me with a fifty-dollar fine for contempt of court—which amount, confidentially, doesn't nearly begin to express my real feelings in regard to the gentleman! The upshot, however, is that you'll have to languish where you are, at least for a while.'

Though disappointed, Gordon was not surprised. O'Dion had the upper hand now, and he intended to keep it, regardless. Should the law be bent and twisted in the process, that was his conception of its purpose.

Supper was brought them, but if any visitors requested admission, they saw no sign of them. Harder had a sound respect for his prisoners, and he did not intend to take any chances.

Gordon sat on the edge of his bunk and pondered, to no good effect. He'd never had much experience with jails, but this one seemed reasonably clean. Beyond that, he could find no good point in its favor. It was solidly built, and escape appeared to be out of the question. They would hold him, on one technicality or another, until it was too late to matter.

Meanwhile, all that he had tried to do would go for naught, and O'Dion would hasten toward a final round-up. Driscoll McKay was dead. He was in jail. Abe McKay was blind. Lomax, again acting foreman in his absence, would be helpless in such an emergency; as helpless as himself, because he'd again underestimated the opposition.

Drake was in the adjoining cell. They discussed the situation, unable to find anything hopeful; then Drake stretched on his own bunk and was soon snoring. Gordon listened, his anger as tight as his clenched fists. It was too dark to see, since no light had been left burning. Except for themselves, the jail and the adjoining sheriff's office were empty. It could be a long night, and he'd do well to follow Drake's example, so as to be fresh should any opportunity develop. There was no profit in worrying or in blaming himself.

The trouble with such advice was that it was easier to propound than to follow. He was tired, but not at all sleepy. Even the barred window was invisible, and when he stood on tiptoe and strove to see out, the town was equally dark. The citizens retired early, after the manner of hibernating animals.

With the town asleep on a wintry night, there was no sound, not even a dog, to answer a coyote on a distant hill. The stillness was as intense as the blackness.

Then he heard a key, turned softly in a lock.

Tensely Gordon listened, sounds coming like muted whispers. Someone was out there, moving in that stygian blackness without a light. Whoever it was seemed to know his way by instinct, to go surely and without difficulty.

Shoes made a soft, shuffling noise; then there was a faint scraping as keys were tried and rejected, until one fitted the lock, this one the lock to his cell. A voice whispered his name.

'Brick—are you awake?'

'I'm awake, Abe,' Gordon confirmed, and allowed pent-up breath to dribble from his lungs.

'Then we'd best be moving.' The observation was matter-of-fact. 'Come on; I'll guide you. Put your hand on my arm. Where is Drake?'

'In the cell right next to mine.'

Drake was awake then, disturbed by their voices, but he refrained from asking questions. More fumbling was required before the right key was found to open his door. Then the three of them moved along the corridor.

'I don't quite get this,' Drake protested. His voice was both doubtful and amazed. 'You do about as well as if you could see where you're going, Mr. McKay.'

Abe's chuckle was amused. 'Better, most likely,' he returned. 'Since I can't see at all, any time, I'm used to moving in darkness. As for this place, I was actin' sheriff here for a few months, a few years ago, so I got to know my way around. Everything's still kept the same, includin' the keys. Which reminds me. You boys will feel better-dressed with guns on.'

He turned toward the jail office. Gordon heard a desk drawer opened, then soft clicks as the chamber of a revolver was twirled, while sensitive fingers made certain that it

149

was filled with loaded shells. Then the gun was handed to him, another to Drake.

'The sheriff has a way of takin' guns away from people, then forgettin' to return them,' Abe explained. 'So there's always a few in here.'

Here, where he had neither looked for nor expected a break, was extraordinary luck. No one but a blind man could have managed what Abe was doing. Even the sheriff would have required a light to move around in the darkness, to unlock doors and guide them, simply because, like most others, he was accustomed to light. Only a man who no longer depended on vision could manage in blackness.

Anyone working with a light would run the risk of it being seen and investigated. On the other hand, no one would even suspect that the jail could be prowled in such darkness.

'Lucky for me Harder didn't lock the outside door,' Abe added casually. 'Mary was plumb upset about them throwin' you into jail. Larry Vick, he's still working, trying to think of some way to help, but I doubt he's having much luck. He told me what our pillars of the law are up to—aimin' to hold court, first thing in the morning, and to throw the book at you. You're giving O'Dion a bad time, and they don't aim to take no chances.'

Such news was not surprising, but the

casual manner in which he had gone about rescuing them was revealing. It explained, at least in part, why O'Dion had restrained his ambitions as long as Abe McKay was actively rodding the Slash. Only when he had been certain that Abe was helpless, and when Driscoll McKay was marked for assassination, had he felt safe in making his play.

'I've sure bungled things, bad,' Gordon gritted.

The fingers which rested lightly on his arm tightened in a reassuring squeeze.

'In a fight, a man usually gets hit just about as many times as he lands a blow,' Abe observed. 'It's the last lick that counts. I like the way you've handled this fight, Brick. You've set Quirt back on their heels, hard. I'd have done things just about the same, if I could have planned it. We at Slash ain't never stood for being pushed around; but we try to live and let live.'

His words were warming, so that the sudden bite of the outer air hardly mattered. The outer door was closing behind them. Long Rain was silent, with no light showing, the hitch rails deserted. High stars gave a faint illumination, which was enhanced by the blanketing snow.

'I'll join Mary and be getting back to the ranch,' Abe explained. 'You'll have plans, I reckon.'

He was gone, fading into the gloom, offering no suggestions for future movements. That was the sort of boss who commanded loyalty, who gave his trust and then backed a man to the hilt. Gordon wished fleetingly that Abe had volunteered some word of advice. But this was his job, and the old man knew, from his own experience, that he was more conversant with the situation than anyone else.

'Gee!' Drake breathed, as they moved ahead. His head-shake expressed both bewilderment and admiration. 'You know, I never guessed that he was really blind—but he's better than most men with eyes!'

CHAPTER FIFTEEN

Gordon would have been glad to share Abe's confidence in his ability. Showdown could not much longer be delayed, but except for that certainty, he had no clear idea as to what his next move should be. It might be morning before the jail break was discovered; when that occurred, the pattern to follow could be readily guessed. He would not merely be branded an outlaw; they would also charge him with the murder of Driscoll McKay. Vick had relayed the word to Abe that they intended to do that, hurrying through a mockery of a trial, then hanging him. Cheated in that, they would offer a heavy reward for him, dead or alive.

Having branded him as fair game, Quirt could join in the hunt, along with the sheriff. Daylight would heavily increase the odds.

The fact that Abe McKay had considered it necessary to set them loose showed how serious he considered the matter. Giving him his freedom, even at the price of outlawry, had been the lesser evil.

Gordon's jaw set, his fingers closing instinctively around his gun butt. As Abe had pointed out, Slash preferred to live in peace, but it didn't stand for being pushed around.

Drake opened the stable door, and they slipped inside, closing it after them. The vague rustlings and stirrings of horses came to their ears; then another sound, this one unexpected: a familiar but aggravated voice.

'Blast it, Curt, we need a light. Nobody's awake anywhere to notice—and what would it matter if someone did?'

'We can't run that risk, not right now,' O'Dion retorted. 'Jenkins is a snoop, and when I asked him if that package had arrived, and he told me he'd turned it over to Gordon, he acted mightily suspicious. Right now, he hasn't much to go on except his own notions. But if he got really stirred up, he's just the sort who'd send in a full report about the whole affair to his boss. And I don't want any nosy inspectors from the post office snooping around. I can handle local law, but the federals could be nasty.'

'Sure, I know that. But we could say that we were in here after our horses. How are we going to find anything in the dark? And for that matter, wouldn't Gordon have kept whatever it was right on him?'

'Harder searched him when he locked him up,' O'Dion returned impatiently. 'He didn't have it, so he must have left it somewhere, and this is the most likely place. That letter said that a package would follow in a few days, containing hard cash.'

In the stress of other events, Gordon had temporarily forgotten about the money. But O'Dion had not; it was very much on his mind. He had apparently been summoned to town after Gordon had been arrested, and he'd risked asking the postmaster about the expected package. Eagerness had caused him to take that chance, since he had been fairly certain that Jenkins would be unaware of recent developments.

Gordon grinned. This was a break he hadn't expected. Still, luck had a way of being impartial. If you were alert and ready to take advantage when the chance came, you were called lucky. When a man failed to do so, he was termed unlucky. Quite often it was as simple as that.

Drake nudged him as a signal, then slipped

away in the gloom. Gordon drew his revolver and carefully eared back the hammer, then took a couple of steps and jammed the barrel against a shadowy figure.

'Reach!' he instructed, while with his other hand he helped himself to the holstered weapon of his prisoner.

Drake was working in unison, surprising Yankus at the same instant. Both men from Quirt were taken without difficulty.

'Now what do we do with such a pair of thieves?' Drake asked. 'We've caught 'em red-handed in the act!'

'Well, I suppose we could take them to the nearest patch of trees and hang them,' Gordon observed, 'seeing that they planned that sort of a welcome to the new day for me.'

O'Dion stumbled into the trap.

'You can't do that, Gordon,' he protested. 'You were to have a fair trial before you were hung.' He started to say more, then stopped, aware that he had betrayed his knowledge of the plan.

'You'd be surprised,' Gordon assured him grimly. 'And after what you've just said, as well as the way you've been carrying on, I'm running out of patience.'

Drake scratched a match and touched the flame to a lantern wick. Rope was conveniently at hand, and he tied their prisoners' hands, then held them under guard while Gordon checked his saddle-bags,

155

making sure that the package of money was intact. Growing desperation was upon the face of O'Dion as well as on Yankus'.

'You can't get away with this,' the latter burst out. 'Our crew's outside—and this time they'll hang you!'

The bluff was so manifest that Gordon did not bother to answer it. Two saddled horses from Quirt had been brought in, and they made the prisoners mount, then ran thongs from their bound wrists to the saddle-horns, leaving them helpless.

'Now we ride,' Gordon said.

There was no sign of anyone else from Quirt, and the remainder of the crew were probably asleep. Being sure of himself, O'Dion had risked a quick trip in to town after receiving a report that Gordon was behind bars. He would keep in the background, while pushing for a swift trial in the morning, making sure that neither his sheriff nor judge failed to hang this rebel before most people even knew what was going on. Once that was done, the war as well as the battle would be won.

Even with fresh horses between their legs, this had the markings of another long night, though it would be more comfortable as far as temperature was concerned. There was a feel of change in the air as they left the town behind, a quality as intangible as a woman's mood, yet definite. Already it had warmed a few degrees, the arctic bite blunted by a returning softness which might have been left over from the summer.

Two courses of action were open. They could return to the Slash, or keep straight on toward New Cheyenne. Despite their having O'Dion as a hostage, either method would bristle with hazards. Striking for the distant town was riskier, but the increasing odds might be balanced by greater rewards. To hole up at the ranch meant a certain clash at arms, and as far as the law and the record went, they'd be in the wrong all the way. The longer course might still avoid a murderous battle of the crews, and that had been his objective from the first. If it was inconsistent that hired hands should die to decide an issue for O'Dion, it was equally so where he was concerned.

O'Dion grunted in surprise when they failed to make the turn to the ranch. Clearly, he had expected nothing else.

'Are you heading for Barclay's?' he demanded. 'Or do you want just to get out of the country? *That* would be sensible.'

'Well, we could keep riding,' Gordon conceded. 'We should come up with the wagons, sooner or later.'

O'Dion gave a snort of laughter.

'If ever you do, you'll be too late, as you've been from the beginning.'

'In that case, what are you worrying

about?'

O'Dion shrugged. 'No worry for me. It's merely that I'm reminded that the wicked flee when nobody pursues. It's just that I hate to see you knock yourself out for nothing, Brick. You should have stuck where you belonged, with Quirt—and it's not too late to change.'

Gordon imitated the shrug. 'With *me* paying you for the privilege—to the tune of thousands? There's a sour note to that.'

The reminder that he knew all about the money left O'Dion without an answer. They moved at a steady pace, putting miles between themselves and the county seat. They were penetrating into enemy country, but it was clear that O'Dion's apprehension was mounting faster than his own. His manifest nervousness reassured Gordon that he was doing the right thing.

It continued to grow warmer, and now a chinook wind was blowing down from the mountains. Rawly cold at sundown, the change became striking. Gordon unbuttoned his heavy coat, noting that Drake was doing the same. The snow underfoot no longer squeaked and rattled with an icy brittleness. It was assuming a soft, almost clinging quality about the hoofs of the horses. No longer did breaths rise and swirl like fog.

So swift a change in the weather seemed like an omen. Gordon had seen the temperatures alter swiftly, though seldom to such an extent. When conditions were right, the thermometer could climb or drop a degree a minute, and tonight it was shifting from below zero to above the freezing point. Occasional small puddles appeared in the road, and tiny streams struggled to cut courses for themselves among the snowbanks.

O'Dion finally raised his voice in protest and supplication.

'Have a heart,' he begged. 'We're cooking, buttoned up in these heavy coats. Either loosen our hands so we can do it ourselves, or help us shuck out of them.'

The request was too reasonable to refuse, though Gordon recalled how uncomfortable he had been while imprisoned in the bear pit. Both men were sweating, their faces beaded with moisture. Gordon rode alongside O'Dion and reached with his free hand to loosen the buttons of the overcoat.

'That helps,' O'Dion muttered, and turned his face to the moon, which until then had been obscured by a haze of cloud.

'Ain't it pretty, now?' O'Dion's mood seemed to have softened, like the air. 'I'll make a guess that you'd rather be ridin' with a certain lady for company, a night like this. Suit me better, too, if you were.' His chuckle covered the sudden convulsive twist of his body as he swung a foot free from the stirrup, reaching, lifting. The rowel of the spur caught at Gordon's gun-belt, and instantly the Quirt boss gave a savage, lunging kick downward.

Frightened, Gordon's horse veered away, and in that moment, O'Dion came close to accomplishing his purpose. The needle-pointed spur had been aimed to puncture like a knife, to tear a wound in Gordon's side. It failed as the horse jerked away, partly deflected by heavy shirt and underwear. Then the slashing bark raked downward along Brick's thigh, tearing cloth and flesh alike, while blood spurted and pain lanced.

The next instant, O'Dion was roweling his horse with both spurred boots, sending it into a wild gallop; Yankus was quick to emulate his boss. That was the moment chosen by the moon to duck back under the cloud.

Desperation lay in such a try at escape, but for a few moments it seemed as though by its very recklessness it might succeed. Both prisoners were shackled by their wrists to saddle-horns, but they still held the bridle reins in their fingers and so were able to control their horses.

Here the valley widened, flattening out, spotted with a scattering of pines and cottonwoods. Among these, much of the snow had been swept clear by the wind, leaving the ground bare, providing easy running for a horse.

With the moon gone, the darkness seemed

thicker than before. Once lost among scores of acres of trees, a fugitive would be hopeless to find.

Gordon pursued, pain lancing along his thigh, his fury mounting with the agony. His gun was in his hand and clear of leather before he could check the wild impulse to use it. The longer reach it would give to his arm would check escape, but the trouble was that he couldn't shoot a man in the back, even an escaping prisoner; particularly not when the man was unable to fight back.

Nor could he blame O'Dion too much for the trick, or the manner in which he'd worked it. Tonight, it was more than Quirt or Slash which was on the board. Their lives topped the gamble, and when the stakes were the sky, all limits were off.

His anger had become brittle as he overtook O'Dion, his horse sweeping alongside. He leaned to grab at the bridle, and again O'Dion spurred, driving his cayuse to a frenzy, sending it rearing, almost breaking loose. Allowing his own horse its head, Gordon grabbed his gun again. Twisting, about, he smashed hard with the barrel.

The clubbed steel caught O'Dion on the skull, raking down along his cheek, leaving a livid track. O'Dion slumped, the fight gone out of him. Drake pulled to a halt to stare.

'You killed him?' he asked.

161

'I wouldn't much mind if I had,' Gordon growled. The pain along his thigh was subsiding to short and savage jolts, but the leg would remain sore for days to come. By the time they returned to the road, O'Dion was able to hold himself erect, riding in sullen silence. When he broke it, his words were baleful.

'They that take the sword shall perish by the sword. So it is written. This now has become a personal matter between us.'

Gordon did not bother to reply. He was listening to a new sound, faint but increasing. The others caught it also, and Drake's face showed concern.

Other riders were abroad, despite the hour—many of them, judging from the muted jingle of bridle bits and the soft thud of hoofs. Men were coming up the road from the south, about to top the slope, and would be upon them almost without warning.

Drake's face smoothed with sudden relief. 'Luck's with us!' he breathed. 'It's our missing crew! That was Lomax's voice!'

CHAPTER SIXTEEN

There was no mistaking the voice. A grating quality set it apart from most others, as though rust had crept into the vocal cords,

162

rust which might be improved by a drop of oil. The tone and words matched.

'When it comes to that, I cut my eyeteeth on the trail from Texas to Arizona, and I was weaned on Chisum's road. I can ride to hell and back if I have to—which is not to say that I like to.'

Drake's face was relaxing, widening to a grin. It hung, wide and vacuous with dismay, as the others topped the rise and were suddenly all around them. This was a big crew who rode by night—twice too many for the missing bunch from Slash.

Lomax was one of them, and the others who had journeyed with him were there. On that count there was no mistake. But they rode as prisoners, and the men who watched the captives were on horses branded with the Quirt.

There was no chance to resist, none to make a break. Within a matter of moments, Gordon and Drake had been added to the list of captives. Almost as quickly, O'Dion and Yankus were cut loose.

O'Dion blinked, then slid from his horse, shaking himself like a dog emerging from water. He looked about, savoring the feel of freedom. Then he strode across to where Gordon was standing, suddenly helpless with his arms twisted behind his back and his wrists already pinioned with a tightly drawn rawhide thong.

'The way of the transgressor—' O'Dion spat, and drove his fist into Gordon's face.

The blow was venom-packed, savage with pent-up hate. Gordon pitched on his back, making a muddy splash into a pool of melting snow. With the same calculated deliberation, O'Dion drove the toe of his boot against Gordon's side. He twisted at that moment, so that his arm deflected part of the force; otherwise several ribs might have been cracked. While he lay, gasping and half-numb with pain, O'Dion set a foot on his chest and held him, staring heavy-lidded.

'That's what you get for hitting *me*,' he observed, then turned away.

Yankus was no less vindictive, rubbing his own chafed wrists. 'Why don't we string the pair of them up and be done with it?' he demanded.

'It may be that we will do just that,' O'Dion returned thoughtfully. 'We shall see whether or not that is as effective as certain other methods. In any case, we should await the proper time. There is a tradition that it comes harder to die at sunrise.'

Sunrise would not be far off. The haze of clouds which had returned when the chinook began to blow were dissipating again, and it would be a fine fall day.

'How did you get hold of them?' O'Dion questioned, indicating the Slash crew with a wave of his hand.

164

'We had a bit of luck,' Yuma admitted. 'We came upon them where they'd camped for the night. It having turned warm and they being tired, they were so sound asleep that we had them before they realized what was going on.'

O'Dion's mood was abruptly jovial. 'They have the look of small boys caught in mischief,' he observed. 'But when a prodigal journeys into a far country, he gets took.'

Chuckling at his own wit, he ordered Gordon lifted from the mud and onto a horse. Gordon had been wondering about the crew and their predicament. With Lomax in charge, they had turned back toward the Slash, while he and Drake had continued on to New Cheyenne. Apparently Lomax had taken it upon himself to swing again toward either the camp or the town. The reason no longer made a difference.

Soaked, mud-encrusted, his face battered and bloody, Gordon made a sorry figure as they again turned about, heading once more for the country of the Bitter Sage. Never had it seemed more aptly named.

It did no good to review the mistakes along the way; some, such as the last, had been impossible to foresee and as difficult to avoid. The total added up to disaster, leaving O'Dion in full control. Some of the Slash riders were still at the ranch, but it would not be hard to surprise them.

Immediate matters had temporarily driven other things from the mind of O'Dion. Now, taking a review of events, memory gave him a pleasant reminder, and he pushed his horse alongside Gordon's. Dawn was spreading, a sudden lightening of the heavier blackness which had closed briefly, as if to help hide the shame of Slash.

'I was almost forgetting something,' O'Dion observed, 'so much has happened this night. But the philosopher observed that joy cometh in the morning.' He made clear his meaning. 'There is the matter of that package sent out from the East.'

At his order, the man who led Gordon's horse halted it. O'Dion himself dismounted to delve eagerly into the saddle-bags. Finding them empty, he scowled in angry disbelief.

'Where is it?' he demanded. 'Now what the devil have you done with it?'

'Done? With what?' Gordon countered. 'Should I be a mind-reader, now?'

'You know what I mean,' O'Dion growled. 'Where's the money?'

'Do you mean the money that was sent me, as an inheritance—by registered mail, as Eli Jenkins will testify—'

O'Dion hit him again, his fist smashing hard against Gordon's mouth, so that he reeled in the saddle, then spat out blood. O'Dion stood a moment, breathing hard, but he did not pursue his questioning. The

166

answers, with men from both crews listening, were worse than embarrassing. They might even prove incriminating.

Again with a change of mood, O'Dion swung to view the horizon, which was beginning to flame in vivid hues as the sun gave notice of its coming.

'I smell the dawn,' O'Dion murmured. 'Dawn—and sunrise. But I might be inclined to make a trade—and if I was in your boots, I would consider any sort of a deal to my advantage.'

Gordon shrugged.

'You've already made sure that I haven't got an advantage,' he pointed out. 'Also, dead men reveal no secrets!'

He thought O'Dion was going to hit him again, but the boss of Quirt restrained himself, conscious of the battery of watching eyes. Disapproval was in the faces even of his own men. Scowling, he climbed back on his own horse. For the moment, it was checkmate. There would be no profit in hanging Gordon, if afterward the money should prove so securely hidden that he could never find it.

A new notion occurred to him. Gordon might well have cached the package somewhere along the line of the night's ride. There had been chances enough.

'It's a long chance you're taking,' O'Dion warned balefully, 'especially while there are higher stakes on the board. And my temper is growing short.'

Knowing that to be more truth than bluff, Gordon made no reply. For the time being the money was an ace, and O'Dion was too greedy to risk its loss merely to satisfy a personal grudge.

Yankus pushed alongside O'Dion with a suggestion, and a halt was called. Wood was gathered, cook fires kindled. It was still a long ride back to Quirt; moreover, the crew of Quirt were equipped with all necessary provisions, in packs tied behind saddles. They had been on the go through most of the night, as well as the previous day. Tired and hungry as they were, there was no need for haste.

The aroma of frying bacon and boiling coffee soon spilled tantalizing fragrances on the air. The captives were untied, with a single exception. Gordon was left with his hands still fastened behind his back, to stand against a tree and watch hungrily while the others ate.

'You have but to say the word, to enjoy breakfast with the rest of us; then you can get on your horse and ride out,' O'Dion observed. 'The choice is for you to make.'

'The price of such a meal would come too high,' Gordon replied.

'Were my own neck in the balance, I should count the cost as cheap,' O'Dion contradicted him, but let it go at that. Gordon was boosted back to the saddle and the ride resumed, the other prisoners tied again. O'Dion was not inclined to take any chances which could be avoided.

'A man's errors may be pardoned seven times,' he commented. 'But there comes a limit both to patience and good-nature.'

'Did you never hear of seventy times seven?' Gordon wondered, and O'Dion scowled and swung away.

It was full daylight, and the untrammeled sun seemed intent on making up for its aloofness of the past couple of days. It was not long before the horses' hoofs were churning the snow to slush. Here and there, tiny rivulets moved to form small streams, and puddles were becoming ponds. Bare spots of ground began to appear, lending the hillsides the speckled appearance of a turkey egg.

So peaceful a ride could not last long. Inevitably they would meet others who were using the roads, and with one crew riding disarmed and under guard, questions would be asked and, sooner or later, a challenge raised. Yet the chance of any serious challenge diminished with each accession of power to the Quirt.

Gordon, bound hands tied behind his back, dried blood and bruises marring his face, took note of the eager watchfulness in O'Dion's eyes as they rode. He was like a ferret, his eyes questing, darting back and forth, calculating, weighing, ever hopeful. The snow was a vast blanket, largely unmarred except for the trail made by the four of them as they had headed the other way. It was that which O'Dion watched, hopeful for any sign which might indicate where the package of bills had been hastily cached during the ride.

Several times the Quirt boss drew off, once to turn over a large flat rock, again to thrust his arm into the hollow of a tree, once to search above an outthrusting branch on another tree. There the snow had been disturbed, a large chunk falling. O'Dion's failure to find what he sought did nothing to improve his temper.

It was mid-morning when they sighted another group of horsemen, heading their way. They continued to come on, with no change in pace, and O'Dion in turn gave no sign or order to slow down. The gap narrowed, vanished, and both sides pulled up by common consent.

Here was Slash, or what remained of the crew; they had been riding to meet them. Having heard of Gordon's escape from jail, they had waited for him to return to the ranch. When neither he nor Drake had showed up, it had been easy to guess where they must have headed, and why.

By the same token, they were likely to need

help. The rest of the crew had set out to try to give it.

Now, faced by a crew twice their own number, they were standing their ground. The trouble was that the odds verged on the hopeless; not only were they outnumbered and outgunned, but Quirt had the advantage of hostages.

As though even that had not not been enough, another group of riders were coming into sight, further to overbalance the scales. At their head rode Sheriff Lem Harder.

CHAPTER SEVENTEEN

Harder came on without a pause, cutting across open range, the horses leaving a sloppy pattern in their wake. The sheriff was no poker player, and an expression of triumph fitted itself to his face like a misshapen mask as he took in the situation, the overwhelming weight of the odds, and the hostages which Quirt held. His glance turned baleful as it fastened on Gordon.

He swung to join with Quirt, pulling up only when his men had become a part of the larger group.

'Good morning, Mr. O'Dion,' he greeted. 'From the look of things, you have done a good day's work already. I was looking for some of them,' he added grimly. 'So I'll be pleased to take Gordon off your hands. The judge is anxious to see him in court.'

O'Dion was savoring his triumph, as a cow savors its cud.

'It will be a pleasure to turn the man over to you, Sheriff,' he agreed. 'I was taking him to town for that purpose.'

Then, the formalities having been observed, O'Dion's patience, never long, grew suddenly thin. He swung in the saddle to scowl upon the remaining crew of Slash.

'Well?' he challenged. 'What do you men want? You wouldn't be looking for trouble, now—or riding with the intention of aiding and abetting known outlaws?' His head thrust forward. 'You're through, on this range—finished—you as well as your outfit. Throw down your guns and ride out, and you have my word that no one will interfere with you. But if you don't—'

He paused, staring challengingly at their leader. A new man filled that role today, one who had suffered frustration the day before and found its flavor bitter in the mouth. Larry Vick was leaving his law books behind for a while, shifting his trust to Judge Colt, because of his contempt for the man who had been shoved into a judge's robes. Somehow, he looked more at home in the saddle than in an office, though he still wore his rusty frock coat. But under its long skirts nestled a

172

holstered gun.

He lounged in the saddle, looking from one group to the other, assessing the odds, studying the situation. Then, surprisingly, he smiled.

'I had thought that the storm was over, but there is still a strong wind blowing,' he observed. 'And while it's words we're bandying, I'll offer a bit of advice, O'Dion. Down Texas way they have a saying that it's a long rope which has no hangman's knot at its end!'

At the implication, O'Dion's face reddened. No one could mistake the lawyer's meaning.

'You may be right,' he barked. 'And some such ropes might well be put to use! Am I to take it, Vick, that you think of yourself as a fighting man? For your own sake, you'd better prove a better one than you managed to be with your law books.'

'If it comes to fighting, I've learned to know one end of a gun from the other.' Vick shrugged. 'However, before anyone resorts to such drastic measures, I've a word for you. It should be enough. It has to do with tampering with the United States mail!'

O'Dion's face went from ruddy to pale and back again. Victory and triumph had seemed complete, and he'd temporarily forgotten about the theft, yet this was the one factor which left him uneasy. Now it was apparent

173

that Eli Jenkins had been wagging his tongue. In effect, Vick was telling him that the postmaster had sent word to some higher-up in the department, and that the federal law was too big even for O'Dion.

As well it might be, O'Dion conceded. But the fool was overlooking one thing. A dead lawyer could push no charges, and once Quirt was in undisputed control of the range, Jenkins would know better than to voice even his suspicions.

In one way, it was not too bad. For days now they had played a grim game, in which Brick Gordon had striven to checkmate him without recourse to force, hoping to avoid a clash in which many would die. On that point, O'Dion had been willing to go along.

There was a saying that circumstances altered cases, and he was ready to accept that. Even a week before, he'd been eager to show his power, at whatever cost. All at once, he stood on a pinnacle of which he'd not even dared dream when coming to the valley of the Sage, the threshold of absolute dominance. From the heights the view was not only wider but different.

As overlord of the range, he'd be somewhat in the position of a country squire, and such a title carried respect—or should do so. The additional spilling of blood was a blot to be avoided if at all possible.

But if the choice was rule or ruin, faced

with hotheads like Vick—then his course was clear. Whichever way had to be taken, he couldn't lose.

'You're a fool, Vick,' O'Dion said cuttingly. 'Did you never hear of the prodigal who wasted his inheritance? You should never leave your books in favor of a gun. But that you have done, asking for a showdown, so it's up to you. If you are eager to lead these hotheads to their death, it's your choice.'

Harder cut in urgently. Affairs seemed to be building to the sort of climax which made him squeamish.

'As sheriff, I call upon you, all of you, to throw down your guns in the name of the law!'

Vick's face had lost color until it almost matched the melting snow, but his voice held as steady as if in a courtroom.

'Go to hell!' he returned.

This was it, and tension was poised at hair-trigger balance. Every man sat poised and ready, and the nervousness or over-eagerness of anyone on either side might precipitate a crisis.

It came whence none had looked for it, sudden and sharp. There was a rapped order in Brick Gordon's voice.

'Reach, O'Dion,' he instructed. 'And think hard, man!'

His hands were no longer behind his back or hidden under the skirts of his long coat.

With attention centered on Vick and O'Dion, no one had noticed as he withdrew his hands, shaking the left arm briefly to free it of the loosened thong, nudging his horse another step with his knees, bringing it alongside O'Dion's.

Gordon's wrists were red and swollen, bruised and chafed, but it had been easy enough to close his fingers about the butt of O'Dion's holstered gun, to draw and jab the muzzle against O'Dion's back.

'Should I squeeze on the trigger, it could be a short, quick journey to where Vick has consigned you,' Gordon added, and the pressure of the gun muzzle was unrelenting.

Dismay and surprise battled in O'Dion's face. He twisted about to stare in disbelief, and met Gordon's grim smile in return.

'It was yourself did it, if that's any comfort to you,' Gordon answered his unspoken question. 'Rawhide draws mighty tight and holds as grimly as the jaws of a bulldog. But rawhide stretches when wet. It was your pleasure to knock me flat on my back, then to shove me deeper in the mud with your boot! But while you held me there, my hands and the rawhide were in a pool of water, where it soaked and stretched!'

It seemed as though no man breathed, and rage flamed higher in O'Dion's face as he understood. His own hand was poised, neither lifting in a token of surrender nor stabbing toward a gun which, he realized with a shock, was no longer waiting to be grasped.

He tried to calculate coolly, for either way lay ruin. Would it be more satisfying to go out in a blaze of gunfire, and not alone? Men who drew their pay gave loyalty to their outfit in return, and these men would follow him even on the long ride. They could turn the day to devastation—

'Here comes Eli Jenkins,' Gordon added. 'And someone's with him—a stranger by his looks.'

O'Dion's gaze shifted as others were doing. No one had seen the little postmaster on a horse for at least a dozen years, yet now he rode, jerkily but determinedly. The other man seemed as little at home in the saddle, but equally determined.

Jenkins looked around, taking in the position and condition of the rival crews, and understanding came into his face. Always pale, it was even whiter now, but he kept straight on to a position between the two groups before pulling up.

'You've lost already, O'Dion,' he greeted. 'Give up. Luck runs both ways, and you've had a lot of the breaks. Mr. Gordon's side got one when Mr. Struthers came to town this morning. He's an inspector for the post office, and he's here to arrest you for tamperin' with the United States mail.'

'That is correct.' Struthers' face was flat

177

and as devoid of expression as his voice. 'I will take him off your hands, sir,' he added to Gordon, 'with your leave.' A pair of handcuffs flashed in the sun, clicking shut like a conjuring trick. O'Dion stared blankly at the manacles in which his hands were encased.

The fight went out of Quirt at the sight. There was much which they did not understand, but two things were clear. O'Dion had lost his gamble, and you did not fight federal law.

In any case, Gordon was in control.

The newly arrived riders from Slash were already at work, cutting loose their fellows. The men from Quirt, making use of their opportunity, began drifting away.

Lomax pushed alongside Gordon, his face showing anxiety as well as relief.

'Are you all right, man?' he demanded. 'You look hard-used. But you made all the difference. If you hadn't moved as you did, everything would have gone up in smoke.'

He was probably right. Gordon, in the moment of reaction, was suddenly very tired, and it came to him that the victory was far from complete. As though reading his thought, Lomax grinned.

'Relax, man,' he said. 'Everything's working out fine—better than we'd a right to expect. We've an airtight case, even to the hides.'

Gordon was beginning to understand. 'So that's what you've been about, eh?'

Lomax nodded, not unpleased with himself.

'I got to thinking, right after we left you,' he admitted. 'You and Drake were going on, risking your necks. Why should the rest of us head back, just to get warm and take it easy? So I took it upon myself to turn about again. We ate some of that veal at the camp—and very good meat it was. Also, we got some sworn statements as to where they had gotten hold of the meat in the first place!

'Then,' he added modestly, 'we swung off and overtook a couple of wagons loaded with hides, not far out from New Cheyenne but headin' off toward Salt Lake—and danged if those hides weren't calfskins, with fresh Quirt burns on them!'

Gordon grinned, too, beginning to catch the contagion of Lomax's mood. Any way you looked at it, these men of Slash would do to ride with.

'What happened to the wagons?'

'We sent them toward Long Rain, but by the lower road,' Lomax explained. 'It's a full day longer, but we figured it might be safer. They should be showing up in town sometime today.'

Not knowing of the transfer of the hide wagons, the crew from Quirt had remained ignorant that their ace had already been

179

trumped. With the hides, the case would be complete, with no loopholes. Not that it was especially necessary, except that Quirt, and whoever assumed its management, would be required to make full restitution.

'Let's get back to the ranch and have something to eat,' Gordon suggested. 'I'm hungry.'

'You do have a hungry look,' Lomax agreed. 'That ain't to be wondered at, after missin' your breakfast the way you did. But if I ain't presumin' too much in suggestin' it—I'd say that you have other reasons just as strong as your stomach, or maybe more so, for getting there. Like tellin' the good news to Miss Mary—and Abe, of course.'

Rewarded by a wave of color which flowed across Gordon's unshaven face, Lomax chuckled and forebore to pursue the subject. Drake, however, had a question.

'If I ain't being too curious,' he said, 'I'd like to know what you did with that package, there at the stable. You fooled me as well as O'Dion on that.'

'You mean the money?' Gordon roused from a pleased reverie. He crossed to where the inspector was preparing to ride with his prisoner and delved into O'Dion's saddle-bags, pulling out the packet before O'Dion's widening eyes. 'It seemed like a good place to put it for safekeeping,' Gordon observed.